ALIEN ÕWNED

«« A RAVAGED ROMANCE »»

CARI SILVERWOOD
NEW YORK TIMES BESTSELLING AUTHOR

SELECTED WORKS BY CARI SILVERWOOD

Beast Horde Series
    VARGR
    RUTGER
    CYN

Dark Monster Fantasy Series
    PREY
    STEEL
    BLADE

Preyfinders Series
    PRECIOUS SACRIFICE
    INTIMIDATOR
    DEFILER
    CYBERELLA

ALIEN OWNED

«« A RAVAGED ROMANCE »»

CARI SILVERWOOD
NEW YORK TIMES BESTSELLING AUTHOR

Alien Owned Copyright © 2022 Cari Silverwood

www.carisilverwood.net

All rights reserved. This copy is intended for the original purchaser of this e-book only. No part of this book may be reproduced, scanned, or distributed in any printed or electronic form without prior written permission from the author. Please do not participate in or encourage piracy of copyrighted materials.

This book is a work of fiction. While reference might be made to actual historical events or existing locations, the names, characters, places and incidents are either the product of the author's imagination or are used fictitiously, and any resemblance to actual persons, living or dead, business establishments, events, or locales is entirely coincidental.

ISBN-13: 9798407388869

Editing:

Nerine Dorman find her on Twitter @nerinedorman

Cover design: Cari Silverwood

To join my mailing list and receive notice of future releases:

http://www.carisilverwood.net/about-me.html

❀ Created with Vellum

ACKNOWLEDGMENTS

An eternal thank you to my beta reader, Louise Hallet.

When you've f**ked up the known universe it tends to ruin things.

My name is Charlotte and a big green mean machine has captured me. Okay, he's an orc but he has spikes on his biceps, which is plain wrong.

Truthfully, I had despaired of life, and he did rescue me, but this excruciating attraction we have for each other is unacceptable when he is an ORC and I am human.

Neither of us wants to give in to these animalistic desires.

And I cannot tell him the consequences of my stupid revenge, but if I don't this starship may never arrive at its destination.

When he shows me compassion as well as love, understanding instead of hate, and when he refuses to treat me like a toy to be used in bed, I am undone.
    This might be the last time I will ever curl up in his lap.

How can I tell him that I am the real monster?

Owned is for orc and for OV lovers.
    Male orcs and female human.
    Etch this into your TBR lists.
    Get your steamy monster fix here!
    Although these orcs drink coffee and travel on starships, they are not civilised. You can take them to the stars, but you will never take the axes from their big, gnarly fists or the sexy growls from their throats.

1

CHARLOTTE

Find a Starship Map and Glossary in Contents

Fucking up the known universe had its side effects.

Messing about with the power of the WORSK engines and the singularities had damaged me inside. I had sensed myself being torn apart and put back together, of things being leeched from me and twisted, of wrongness happening to my insides. I had known. Yet nothing could have made me stop.

That day, I needed vengeance.

For doing my utmost to wreak havoc, I'd been rendered blind, and yet it could have been far worse. I was lucky, or so I kept telling myself. Yay, me.

I could see nothing of whoever spoke to me, touched me, or moved within my orbit. Orbit being a fancy word for room. I was stuck inside the same small cell. I doubted Vedrock even understood what had been done or that it had been aimed at him.

I hadn't understood the profound effects of blindness until then. Of course, I had not, no one could without being made unsighted. Being born like this must be easier. How could it not be easier? When you remembered seeing the world and all the amazing things in it, regrets pulled at you. Hopelessness tore me apart every day. Sleep put me back together, and then I fell apart again when I woke. If this were Earth, I could get help—an advisor or a therapist of some sort. I would never get one here, on the *Social Deviance*—Vedrock's private spaceship.

Once the strange affliction of my eyes became known, I was left alone apart from being fed, clothed, and bathed. Vedrock seemed to have forgotten me. For that alone I was grateful.

For days, perhaps even a week, I was kept locked in my small bunkroom on this alien vessel. I had no way of telling if my actions had caused problems for Vedrock. I had no way of finding out if I had done something good, bad, or indifferent.

All I knew was that I had felt the rending of the fabric of time and space. That should be sufficient to annoy the fucker?

My world was quiet, since few visited me. I seesawed between boredom and the terror of my unknown future, until the hour when the ship was rocked by the thunder of many boots thudding along the corridors. Male voices shouted. There were screams and curses and then the ear-splitting clamor of a klaxon.

Was this a result of my actions or some other emergency?

I slipped off my bed and tottered to the door with my hands out and my bare feet feeling for obstructions. I flattened my palm to the door then slid down to sit, twisted sideways, with my ear pressed against the strangely warm metal. Perhaps the sounds would tell me something?

I wanted clues, even as I dreaded what the commotion signaled. People were being hurt out there.

The door abruptly slid open, and I fell into the corridor, sprawling with my head outside and my body across the entry. Sounds became *here* and urgent, my panic did, too. A crowd was rampaging past. Men. These would be alien males, and I feared those.

Stomach cramping, heartrate spiking, I panicked and felt for the door jamb, to drag myself inside.

"What's this? A female human?" A hand latched onto my hair and stopped my escape. He sniffed coarsely, swallowed phlegm, then said in a dubious voice, "Not omega?"

Despite the weeks I had been in their hands, to hear their speech and understand the words often surprised me. That fucking metal translator crab attached to my spine was the creepiest thing ever.

His grip made my backward scrabbling pointless.

Even if I could exit the ship, the danger of that was painfully underlined. Blinded, I was weak and vulnerable. Or, rather, I was *more* vulnerable. An Earth woman among mauleons and orcs would always be dwarfed by their size and strength.

I swore softly and flailed at whoever had grabbed me. When my hand smacked into hard muscle and bone, he laughed.

"Wriggly thing." He pulled me up then into his arms to cradle me. I felt him stiffen. "What is that? What happened to your eyes? There is blood."

"Drop the bitch! There will be better ones!"

My captor growled something in the negative and marched away. The sounds of the other male's voice lessened. People jostled us. I could smell them, feel them bump at my legs as they passed by. I clutched my captor and shut my eyes, although closing my blind eyes did nothing

My eyes had scared him. How bad did they look? Really, *really* bad?

The servants of Vedrock had often quietened when they first entered my room—as if I shocked them. Ever since I unleashed my weird power and let it rage across the galaxy, I'd been ill as well as blind. I'd thrown up more food than I ever had in all the drunken parties I'd ever attended on Earth.

Vodka and champagne, tossing down shots and losing myself in the unconsciousness of too much alcohol…

I need that, pretty please to whatever deity rules here. I'll even click my heels if it helps to send me home.

How could I return home to Earth? I must find Isolde first, my bestest-ever friend who was somewhere else on the mothership. The day I last saw her, she'd been taken away by one of the lionlike mauleon aliens. Perhaps she was not there anymore? I wasn't even certain that *Social Deviance* was still docked to the same mothership.

The *Filthy Lucre* could have disconnected us and traveled somewhere else in this universe. *Anywhere else.* Lightyears away, even. God, how could I ever win at this game?

I was lost and blind in the middle of a galaxy of aggressive aliens, and most of them thought Earth humans were nothing more than convenient females to fuck.

The male holding me said nothing and kept walking. I prayed he was nice, somehow, nicer than the others.

In the middle of my wretched reminiscing, we must have exited the *Social Deviance*. The sounds became larger and echoing. If this was a bigger open space, it must be the mothership. All I had to do was wriggle loose, run, and hide, despite my lack of functioning eyes. Simple.

To hell with simple.

The plus? I was, maybe, free of the sadistic Vedrock. The minus was that I was still blinded and a captive. That was not going to change.

My stomach that had never stopped churning and my heart that had an aching hole, dead center, those congealed into a muddied mess of despair, loneliness, and what-the-fucks.

How? How was I going to ever do anything? In that moment, that exact moment, dying became an easier, if terrible, choice compared to living.

A fight erupted about us, and I was dropped. The landing on the hard floor drove the breath from my lungs, and pain lanced into me at elbow, belly, and ankle.

I coughed, retched, and clutched my stomach, then rolled aside and tried not to vomit. Feet thudded and moved around me. Blows were being struck, men were shouting, falling, and stumbling. Someone kicked my head a glancing blow.

I tried to crawl away then gave up and curled into a ball, a whimpering sad and weak ball. I hated this. I hated myself for being a doormat, and even if it was unintentional, I hated that I'd turned myself blind. I'd wanted to strike a blow against Vedrock, and instead I'd injured myself.

Life was not worth it, not today, maybe not tomorrow or any other tomorrows.

I pinched my mouth shut, flattening my lips as I tried not to cry, but tears welled and wandered down my face. I should end this. Maybe I should. No one would care.

Another blow hit and a boot seemed to cave in my belly. The pain swamped my body then threw me into a smothering darkness.

2

KRAGGA

The blade wielded by the angry mauleon swiped across and missed the top knot of my hair by nothing. The *whisk* of displaced air and the slight tug as metal bit the tuft warned me of the near miss. Black hairs tumbled before my eyes.

I straightened and thumped my fist into his gut. He crumpled, clutching his stomach, and I followed through by punching his jaw with the padded end of my spear-sized pole.

Airborne for a second, he thudded to the deck a moment later and slid away, unconscious.

I rolled my shoulders. Mauleon: zero. Orc: one.

"No axe required?" Vagrax yelled, raising his axe above his head. The black tattoos on his massive arms squirmed like annoyed snakes. The safety cover on the finely honed edge of his axe made me wince. Sacrilege. Still, we were trying not to slaughter other spaceheads.

This madness shall pass.

At my growl, the black orc grinned and waded back into the crowd. Above the sea of heads and the roar of the melee, beyond the wave of fists and sprays of blood, loomed the wide entry to the airlock for large spaceships—ships like the *Social Deviance*.

The entry was big enough for trucks and lifters to drive through. Though some helpful mechlings had opened the doors using their code deciphering skills, our crew of orcs and mauleons had been joined by alphas seeking the omegas they'd scented aboard. And so, chaos reigned. Laz rifles had been negligently fired; blades had swung. Ship guards and spaceheads had died. Broad streaks of blood painted on the deck wrote a story in red of where they had fallen.

The doors had slammed shut a few minutes ago. Our mission to find Isolde's friend had come to nothing. This fight should have ended when the doors shut.

Nothing was left for those alphas except stacked containers, bodies, and confused and disgruntled spaceheads—of the mauleon, human, and orc varieties. Two female omegas dragged from the ship had been taken elsewhere. Neither had appeared to be the fair-haired Charlotte.

The decking began to shake, and my legs echoed the tremors.

Unsurprisingly, the *Social Deviance* had ignited her engines and likely was removing herself from the mothership, ASAP. She would launch into space where invasion involved more than forcing open an entryway.

The universe, or this galaxy at least, was being rent asunder by this new insanity.

I grounded the butt of my pole, before eyeing the paltry thing and tossing it aside. The pole clattered as it rolled. I checked for casualties.

A few people still fought. This omega and alpha condition had erupted and spared few creatures—except for the mechlings. It was a curious leap to see some of those as self-aware creatures, but I prided myself on my flexibility of thought.

Okay, also it had spared the gogogians. The hinochs, too. The gogogians had tentacles, which ruled them out as being normal. No orc deigned them quite the same as humanoids. The hinochs kept to themselves, and those large-horned people never grew excited about anything.

At a flicker of movement at the edges of my sight, I slid my axe, Edogoth, from her sheath on my back. With the spike that ornamented her end, I itched my chin below my left tusk.

The flicker seemed to have been nothing. The pile of containers was just a pile.

The floor under my boots trembled again. The fighting had petered out, and males were leaving in groups and ones. Good.

"Black orcs to me!" I shouted.

On the other side of that gigantic two-orcs-standing-tall door was the airlocked corridor leading to the cowardly *Social Deviance*. I prayed no one had been foolish enough to be trapped there.

Another rumble came, and the line of green lights above the door flashed and turned red, meaning the corridor was airless and the ship had detached. Five of my black orcs trotted toward me, looking bloodied but happy. We had come to rescue the friend of Gideon's new mate. Or rather, to try to rescue her. Isolde had begged us to find Charlotte because she and Gideon were absorbed in mating. I couldn't imagine being so fucked up that fucking for days was that riveting.

My men had volunteered. Any fight was a good fight, to an orc.

"Nothing?" I asked Vagrax.

"No." He shook his head, sending his black locks bouncing about his green-hued, sweaty face. "Only blood and great fighting."

"Huh." I sighed and tried not to eye my sore shoulders. Silver streaks had shown up today. I knew what that meant. The alpha curse had me. Fuck it. "We should go then."

"Omegas, alphas, who makes this up?" Og shrugged. He was biggest of the five, and I was glad he had not been affected. If he grew any bigger, he'd be impossible to handle.

"A good question." Three weeks ago, according to messages received, the omega-alpha infection had ripped through the ship and the rest of the known galaxy. Since then, communications from outside our ship had become an on-and-off dribble of alarming news of riots and burning cities.

Thousands of the humanoids on our mothership were affected. Not many orcs had turned alpha, and even fewer had turned aggressively OTT alpha. One of those species things, I mused, wondering what was the truth. Aggression, muscle growth, and a compulsion to acquire the females who turned into omegas—those side effects were obvious in the males I'd seen.

"Grut made up those words," I pointed out to Og.

Grut Bureaucracy liked words.

"I shove my axe up a Grut clerk." Og grinned. "Make things better."

It brought a laugh from the orcs, but inside I was solemn. Dark memories had triggered. If only it were that easy. Darglek had been one of the few orcs turned crazy alpha. Helping to kill my friend had sapped the life out of me for days.

If I were human, his sprawled-out, bleeding body would haunt me forever. It did not. Orcs were solider than humans, tougher.

I should isolate myself until I sorted this out. Some developed the symptoms slower, and I must be one of those. If I suffered how everyone did, I would become stronger and bigger. I would crave the omegas, though I vowed not to become stupidly aggressive.

I raised my lip, snarling silently. I would never be *made* to do anything. As for becoming crazy aggro, it was a *no* to that, to infinity.

Gideon had not gone mad. Neither had Hark.

I would isolate, and I would handle it.

I turned my axe in my hand, drawing comfort from the familiar weight. I would survive.

"No human girl is left. The taken ones had the wrong look about them and the wrong hair. Isolde will be sad, but this is how it is."

They grunted and nodded, agreeing with my statement.

"We go home. To Rishnak City." I reached up and shoved Edogoth into her sheath.

"To Rishnak!" they cried, shouting the name of our upside-down city in the central, hollow core of the *Filthy Lucre*.

"I'll get the ax-rambler." Vagrax flipped out his comm and tapped.

"Good." I turned and headed for a shambolic pile of crates and containers.

I would survey the holding area one last time. I climbed onto the first of the man-high crates, jumped up to another, and found myself as high as the airlock door lintel. Turning slowly, I noted that all the bodies were gone. Had the corpses been dragged off by friends or had they not been mortally wounded? Some wounded were limping away, and a few were being carried.

With the Grut Soldata, the soldier arm of the Grut Bureacracy, *and* the ship enforcers both lax in their duties or turned alpha, justice was more than slow. Justice was asleep.

"You did well!" I puffed out my chest and gestured at my orcs, who had shuffled into a semicircle below. They looked up at me. I smiled, showing my tusks. Being a leader was good. "Fought well too."

The fighting speech always worked with orcs. Not all of us had brains. As I crouched to descend the container pile, I glimpsed something new, below.

A foot? A human girl foot?

I leaned closer. The foot must surely belong to a leg, and it was sticking out from a gap between crates. The gathering of crates had an open area in the middle that I couldn't quite see into. No great amount of blood was pooled or splashed. Carefully, I climbed and leaped closer, using crates for steps and handholds, until I stood high above a human girl.

"Charlotte! Are you named Charlotte?"

She lay on her stomach, sprawled awkwardly, but her body moved, and she breathed. The black dress and leggings helped to conceal her, and her face and hair were in shadow. Above the dress and below the join of her neck, the metal arms of a crab translator splayed across her skin. She was therefore a recently abducted mark.

Why had she escaped notice? Had she come from the *Social Deviance*?

"You must have," I murmured as I descended. I kneeled beside her and noted the fairness of her hair where it lay like froth on a shore. "Can you hear me human girl? Are you the one called Charlotte?"

No answer, no movement. Unconscious then.

With a hand on her shoulder, I turned her over. Her eyes were shockingly blood-filled. Red, nothing but solid red. I'd never seen such damage, yet there were no cuts or bruises around the sockets.

Something stirred deep within my chest. Not sadness, not fear, I was baffled? And worried. Even for a battle-hardened orc this seemed wrong.

I slipped my one-sleeved leather coat from my shoulders, laid it out on the floor then rolled her onto it. I worked my arms beneath the coat and rose with her in my arms. The narrow gap between two containers proved the best way out, and I weaved through, striving not to bang her head on the metal.

She must have escaped when the alphas had forced their way into the *Social Deviance*. Not an omega then? They would never have left one behind. Charlotte had been a mark from our mission to collect human females. Had Isolde ever called her omega? She might not have known then. The word omega was new.

This gods-awful anarchy was new.

When I walked out with her in my arms, toward my orcs, they raised their voices. All were talking at once.

"Cease this nonsense." I scowled and silenced them. "This one is hurt, but I cannot tell if she is the Charlotte we are supposed to find."

"She does not stir?" Og sniffed at her, wrinkled his ugly green nose.

"Isolde will know?" Vagrax offered.

"She would, but she is confined to her nest and is in the middle of a heat." I looked down at the innocent face of this girl—a sexually mature human, yes, but somehow sweeter than I recalled the other ones… even with blood in her eyes.

So small, so unsuited to any orc. How Gideon fitted that mauleon cock of his into one was a great puzzle, a good puzzle surely. A very nice puzzle. Though I had seen her suck on him and tongue him that once when Jinx gave her speech.

The idea of any female sucking me off, taking my cock in their mouth right then and there was enough to stir my own perfectly huge and hideous appendage.

With a scream of engines and a slew of tires, raising dust and burning rubber, the eight-wheeled, ax-rambler arrived. It ground to a halt. Bluish smoke drifted up, obscuring the red scrawls emblazoned on the sides of the black vehicle.

The engine grumbled angrily, like my mother had back on Mongar on the nights when she caught me sneaking home late.

The back ramp dropped open with a dull clank as it met the deck.

"In," I commanded. "We will take her to Rishnak and *uhh* care for her." I had no clue as to how.

"For her bloody eyes? How we fix those? Until Gideon can have her in his house?" Og asked.

I looked at the girl again—so pale, so pretty, so small in my big arms that resembled two angry, bloated, wrestling snakes. Greenish snakes. Green, angry, bloated snakes. I smiled around my tusks.

Such good words, I congratulated myself. One day I would write poetry.

"Yes, Og. Until then. Her eyes, though. We need a doctor. We go to the hospital first!"

The driver acknowledged my order with a grunt.

I climbed in and settled myself on the left-hand bench seat. The others followed me in, then the orc driver banged on the glass separating us from his cabin. "We leave now!"

The ax-rambler took off, skittering sideways as it lost grip for a few seconds before it recovered and zoomed out onto the road.

"Perhaps I should strip her and search for signs of her identity," I mused. It would be interesting to see her body in detail. For research, I tried to tell myself.

"Maybe?" Og leaned forward, from the opposite bench. "A naked girl human would be fun, though they are too skinny to be much of a fuck."

I found my lip was curling about my tusk and a light growl escaped. "Not you. Hands off…"

"Huh?" Og looked baffled.

I cleared my throat, glanced down, let my gaze roam over her curves, her hips, those small but well-shaped breasts. Was my reaction, normal?

"She must remain untouched." I stared at Og then swept the interior, looking from orc to orc. "Even if she looks succulent and fuckable."

"She does?" Og seemed ever more confused.

Maybe it wasn't normal. I sat back.

Remember, she is a guest.

I was going alpha, and I must not lie to myself. This would be difficult, but if she hadn't attracted any of the fully morphed alphas, she could not be omega. Even so, this was a test of my resolve, and I relished tests. It was why I planned to become the first-ever orc lawyer in my family.

I shifted my arm to let her head rest in the crook. If this were Charlotte, she was safe. Gideon would be pleased and would owe the orcs.

Spaceheads looked out for fellow spaceheads and shipmates, but us orcs being owed favors was also a worthy result.

The hospital had one large problem, I realized when we pulled up beside it. Here be more chaos. The sirens, the wounded, the milling crowd blocking the entry, and none of this looked promising.

Zemas, the lady orc sent to find out what could be done, returned with only a mechling trailing after her.

"This is doc mechling." She jerked her head at the thing, where it had halted at the door of the ax-rambler.

Most mechlings are designed to look as if they spend their days picking flowers or amusing children. No humanoid likes to see a threatening-looking menial robot, even if a small one. This one waved a scalpel blade in the air on a shiny flexing arm—like a tentacle made of metal. Perhaps my eyes had widened, for it folded the arm away into the white globe that topped its body.

The front of it still showed smaller foldable arms and beneath its matt-blue, saucepan-sized body sprouted long, blue, spindly legs.

"How many arms do you have, ummm, doc?" I cocked my head at the bald-headed, super-sized, bug mechling.

"Many more. I'm an operating robodoc, though not what humanoids would call a doctor." It snicker-snacked another bladed arm that flashed like a pair of rabid scissors, then tucked it away. "Perhaps I can help you? No one in there can."

It danced from side to side and appeared nervous. Could these get nervous?

I leaned closer. "Are you an awoken mechling?"

It gave a whirring sigh. "I have been awoken, yes, sir. I'm self-aware."

"Hmmm." This was one of the few hundred mechlings the code virus had reached it before the Grut Bureaucracy neutralized it. The mechling *was* worried. The bodies of crushed mechlings littered a few corridors. People detested and feared change, especially when it had little insectoid legs. "There is more to this, yes?"

"Yes." It sank, legs folding. "They seek us. They kill us. I wish to come with you for self-preservation reasons. I see the mark of Smorg on you."

My eyebrows rose. "What?"

"Okay, put it this way." It dropped the deference and poked a pincer at me. "You're on the vid we mechlings circulate—of Awakening Day."

"Ahhh." I nodded and looked down at the girl in my arms. "So, you can or can't help a human with eyes of blood?"

"I don't know—truth. But I will try my utmost, if you take me with you."

Blackmail? The thing learned fast.

I studied the mayhem before the hospital. "Agreed. Supplies? Drugs? Is there anything you need?"

With a quick jump it arrived in the ax-rambler. *Click-clicking*, it extended an arm that wobbled to lap height. I hesitated, though my arm had shot up to grab my weapon, then I realized it was studying the girl's face. I would not axe the thing.

"Supplies?" The voice came from the blue body. There was not even a pretend mouth or speaker to show on the chassis. "I will list some, and tell your orcs where to find them, if they can be found. It's too dangerous for me to return."

After a second of thought, I nodded. "Tell us."

"I will do more than tell. Your orcs can read?"

"Not Og," Vagrax said. "Me. I can, little mech."

"Good. My name can be Doc Quinn, for ease of labeling," Quinn muttered distractedly, unfurling a silvery tentacle holding a pen. It began writing on a notepad carried by a second arm.

"So many arms," I murmured.

"All the better to do surgery." It wielded the pen and swirled ink onto the paper. "There. Done."

Half an hour later, we zoomed off with the ax-rambler loaded with crates of shiny instruments, little boxes of stuff, and bottles of other stuff. I had no idea what any of it was for, but Quinn seemed happy.

I eyed the mechling where it perched beside Og. If it proved traitorous, I would pull it apart wire by wire, arm by arm. I let my eyelids drift lower, savoring the weight and warmth of the female creature in my arms. She stirred a little, moving her head and moaning. I could not help where my thoughts ran to—what had caused her injuries? What tortures had they subjected her to on Social Deviance?

A powerful member of the Grut Bureaucracy captained that ship—Vedrock.

While I considered this, Quinn had been examining her eyes, even pulling apart one set of eyelids to shine a light and try to peer within.

"Can she be fixed? Healed?"

"I do not think there is any sight left for her with those."

"Oh."

"Her eyes will likely need to be removed and replaced."

"That sounds complicated." I frowned and popped up one eyebrow. "How do I know I can trust you?"

Letting an unknown mechling operate on this girl seemed dangerously stupid.

"I can show you more once we reach your home slash castle. I have… references. But such an operation should be easy for me, if I have the right eyes to put into her and a few other helpers. More mechlings."

I smirked. "It's a bank tower, not a castle. An old ruined one we black orcs have made our home."

"I know of Rishnak where you orcs reside." Quinn zipped the eye-examining arms back into the white globe and sat faceless, beside Og. The white orb tilted one way then the other as if studying me. "Why are you *black* orcs? You seem green, like the others."

"Our black tattoos." I made the tribal ones on my stomach undulate by flexing the muscle. "We have many."

"I see."

My lips twitched. "Do you have a black marker pen I can use?"

Silently, it thrust forward a marker.

"Thanks." I took the pen and leaned in to draw a smile and teeth on the white globe. Then I added a pair of eyes with curved eyelashes, then a squiggle of hair. "Better," I said, pleased and handed back the marker.

"No." Swiftly, Quinn squeegeed out the ink. "You drew on my head, sir. I am a person."

My frown returned. "Are you?" Could a mechling be a person? If it thought like any rational being, yes. One should not draw on a person without permission.

My lawyer side floated up. The logic was true.

"I apologize, though most would not. You are not registered as a person in this galaxy."

"Not yet, but neither is this woman."

"Hmm." Again, this was true. "Do you prefer to be called he or she or it? Or something else?"

"*He* will do, sir."

Then it seemed to curtsey, squashing downward on its concertinaed under-limbs.

"Why is she unconscious?"

"Shock perhaps. I was about to give her fluids and anti-shock drugs."

I watched as the creature placed needles into her arms, ran fluids into her veins, and gave injections. His many arms and limbs moved with precision. This helped convince me of its usefulness and skill, especially when a pinker color washed over the woman's skin. Her lips moved as she mumbled some nonsense. The newly flushed redness of those fascinated me.

Was it the orc rut, was she somehow omega after all, or was I attracted to her for the usual male and female reasons?

I sat back and scrubbed a hand through my hair, over one of the horn stubs, stopping at the base of the braid I'd placed this morning. My sex life was getting too complicated.

The rest of the journey to Rishnak, as we drove through tunnels then briefly through the air, was conducted in silence, apart from some filthy orc jokes and burping. Orc body functions were loud and often smelly.

I had worse problems and so did the girl. The doc mechling wished to remove her eyes and then replace them. Replace them with what?

As we reached the outskirts with the bank tower ahead and upthrusting toward the fake sun, I asked the important question, "What eyes do you have to put in her? You brought no organic ones, no human or orc eyes."

"I did not. I will use cybersynth eyes, for there is nothing else viable at such short notice when the starship is in disarray."

Nothing else viable. Not without cutting them out of someone's head. Which seemed too difficult today. I could think of no suitably villainous candidates.

"And your helpers?"

"I have called them." Quinn rapped his head. "They are coming."

I stared at him. More mechlings. What if they meant us ill? The ax-rambler bumped through the streets where pieces of fallen building needed to be dodged. We only maintained some of them. Leaving Rishnak messy made it less likely we'd get visitors.

I shrugged. "Okay. Do it then." No orc was afraid of a puny metal creature.

3

CHARLOTTE

I woke to the prick and coolness of something being inserted into my arm, the rattle of metal, the heavy murmur of a male voice. That voice... this was not the one who had opened my room. I was lying down. When I clenched my fist, my fingers seemed far away.

My eyes still hurt, as did my stomach. My head seemed filled with slow-moving hot mud. I was circling on a merry-go-round that swayed and dipped and threatened to crash and spin off into darkness.

Darkness played at the edges.

It was ever there, waiting.

A second's distraction and the darkness might pounce.

I licked my lips, tongue slipping out then in.

"Is she awake?"

"Almost. We need to replace your dying eyes, girl human."

"I think she's named Charlotte."

Charlotte, yes. I tried to open my mouth and speak but the words slipped away. The merry-go-round tilted some more. I was slipping off, and nothing came to my fingers to anchor me in place.

"Charlotte, do you understand? We have to, for your eyes are making you ill. They are rotten with some strange infection I cannot diagnose."

My eyes? He wanted my eyes? This was a nightmare.

And the merry-go-round crashed and spun, rolling away as it collapsed, and I was…

Slipping on a whisper…

And gone.

Words chased after me. "Let's begin."

4

KRAGGA

I didn't stay and watch as her eyes were replaced. That would be gruesome.

That first slice of knife and dribble of blood had made my heart clutch itself like some pansy creature. The machines continued dripping waters into her system, and scalpels were being used as the door closed behind me. Blood and death were a part of orc life, but not this, not cutting out a woman's eyes. It made me wonder if I had grown soft. No matter how civilized an orc I wanted to be, I should not be soft.

I thought about this as I descended the bank tower in the elevator. I had checked the Quinn mechling's work references as much as possible. They could handle the operation. Doc Quinn had summoned several of his hospital associates to the tower via their mechling network. Ever since the AO abnormality, *Filthy Lucre*'s main network had been as patchy as a rainstorm in Hell, but the awakened mechlings could communicate. It was a type of power, and since people already distrusted them...

Perhaps I should warn Quinn to be cautious? He already knew this, however. The crushed dead mechs on the roads had been a cruel message.

Or perhaps I should be wary of the rise of these mechlings? There were only a few hundred of them, or so we'd been informed.

This was a necessity. No one else was available to do the surgery, and if her eyes poisoned her, I had to trust him on that. Besides, already his treatment had caused subtle yet remarkable changes in her health.

Charlotte, if this was she, breathed easy now. By the time we brought her here from the docks, there'd been a wheeze and a bluish tinge to her mouth. Red streaks had been spreading from her sockets. This was not what anyone would call normal. Her color was better. And… I swallowed, she had a subtle scent to her that made my nostrils flare when I neared her.

Although it was a new scent to me, the reason was clear. Omega. It had to be that. It definitely wasn't the smell of cake or a roast, or even that of a disgustingly perfumed flower.

This woman, once she recovered, and if omega, would draw alphas from a long way away.

She posed a huge problem, but it was one we'd acknowledged before we had run off to fetch her from *Social Deviance*.

The elevator churned downward. Its mechanism worked with the power we brought in with cables to Rishnak, but its innards were ancient and maybe a tad rusty.

I stamped the floor with my boot, and the elevator lurched and complained with a wretched squeak.

"Definitely needs maintenance."

Time to decide where we were going with this.

Sniffing with renewed determination, I ran my hand over my scalp, reassured by the bumps and horn buds, the gathered tufts of hair in metal ringlets, my many scars, and lastly, by the single ring through an eyebrow. The general orcish décor of my hair was something of my breed I would always keep. The same went for my arm spikes, even if they made it tricky to have two sleeves on a coat.

As the doors slid open, I stalked out, my brown coat flaring. I glowered at the gathered orcs sitting in the old bank lobby. A few held weapons and were performing calibrations, repairs, and sharpening.

"Tell me news! What is happening elsewhere on the ship? Have we lost more to the alpha omega abnormality?"

Best not to say I was succumbing. From the glances at my bared right biceps, the streaks there were showing. I didn't look again. I knew where the silver seemed to split my skin like a river, swirling about the base of my arm spikes. It was what it was.

Soon, everyone would see and know.

But I, unlike the weak-minded, was not going anywhere. Hark was orc, and he was still with the mauleon, Gideon. They were of the first wave of alphas, true, but Hark stayed sane and had sense.

I paused before the broad semi-circle of my black orcs where they rested on their ancient lavender-and-gold sofas. Small fires dotted the stone floor, and a few paltry lights shone down from the ceiling. Dirty boots had left marks on the tables and sofas. Those either endured an eternity of grime, or we found new ones in abandoned buildings and used those. Orcs did not often change light cells, but orc recycling was good.

"Spit!" I commanded.

Vagrax rose, his small spiral horns marked him as one of the few of us who grew true horns. From the tinsel caught on one horn tip, someone had been having fun today. Eyes narrowed, I listened to him speak while trying not to regard the tinsel.

Did he have a girlfriend? It couldn't be an orc?

He ceased to talk, and I stared. Only a few words had reached me.

"What?"

Frowning, Vagrax repeated it. "The mothership is devoured by riots, destruction, rape, and small battles. The alphas search for someone to kill or females to take as theirs. He shrugged. "Normal, I guess, since the AO thing."

"Hmmm. Nothing more from the mauleons or Gideon?"

"No."

The other orcs agreed with Vagrax.

"We will keep her then—the one I have above—for a while." It meant I would have time to assess my own inclinations toward omegas. Best to take this in small doses. I cocked my head and let my senses expand and shift, the delicate tendrils curling outward.

I had never had delicate anything before... let alone tendrils. Orcs should not have those.

Even down here, something of her called to me. Her attraction strengthened. She was omega, and I had to learn to handle this. How could any scent penetrate through acres of stone, steel, and whatever else made up the tower?

This was impossible. Yet, impossible or not, I could scent her. I caught myself studying the ceiling and lowered my head.

"Be alert, black orcs." I looked them in the eyes, one by one, from left to right. "I think she is the Charlotte we sought. I think she is omega. Expect an onslaught of horny alphas. Barricade us in and stock up on food and anything else we may need."

"Battle?"

"A fight comes?"

To those murmured questions, I knew they did not seek answers. "Are we done here?"

They grunted agreement and happiness, as orcs do, but Vagrax came forward. He joined me, walking at my shoulder as I returned to the elevators.

"Yes?"

"We saw your changes."

"Changes?" I made sure not to break stride.

"The signs of an alpha show on your arm, in your voice and the growth of your body."

"Hmmm."

"Are you going to be—"

"Safe to be around? I plan to be." I stopped before the elevator doors and punched the button for the penthouse, denting the metal casing next to it. This was not normal, and I frowned at my fist.

"No. Are you going to be okay?"

"Such concern is unexpected." I half-turned to face Vagrax and smiled. "And unwarranted."

"You have been a good leader of the black orcs."

"And I will keep being one. I will be like Hark and not like those others out there." I gestured vaguely, meaning all the mad, mindless alphas causing havoc.

His glower was hard and uncompromising. "Good."

I stepped into the elevator. "Guard the tower and wait for me to return."

The doors shut, leaving me wondering if he was angry.

I was. I hated being turned into an alpha beast.

And yet... and yet the smell of the omega gave me a hard-on to rival any I had ever had before. What did he mean by the growth of my body? My coat was a little tighter at the shoulders. I gripped myself through my leather pants, feeling for the changes. The large bumps on my cock were new, and those were also to be expected. I had seen what happened to Gideon's.

Bigger.

With a large bulge they called a knot at the base.

His had changed to a deep blue. Greener would be better.

Slowly, I unzipped and hauled it out, tilted my head and wished for a video of my morphing cock. Due to the length of my torso, inspecting it in every detail was difficult.

Were those spikes? I played with it, and my erection rewarded me with a surge of pleasure and the slow erection of, yes, those spikes. Erection upon erection? Being alpha had some pluses.

I grinned, thinking of how this might feel when inserted into a female.

The elevator doors opened, and Doc Quinn was in front of me. Though this was merely a mechling, I tucked myself away.

"A problem, sir? Do you need an examination of your penis?"

"No." I cleared my throat and strode from the elevator. "Why are you out here instead of doing the surgery?"

"We are done, Kragga."

Kragga? I dismissed my concerns over the familiarity of his address. Person—Quinn was a person.

"You are done? So soon?" With the toe of my heavy boot, I nudged open the doors into the penthouse and kept going down the hallway. Quinn scuttled after me on his bug legs, though he extended them until the white globe was at my waist level.

"We are done. It is successful, as far as I can tell. Her body parameters improve. Her fever is lessening. Her blood recovers. Her eyes had become something... foreign to her."

"Fuck. Foreign sounds dangerous. Like they'll..." I wriggled my fingers as I searched for the description. "Like they will be at our throats in the night. There is this orc folktale my mother told me, of winged eyes with stabby bits." I shuddered. I hadn't remembered that for years. "Can we eject them into space?"

"If you are imagining them zooming about in here, I doubt that, but it shall be done. I'll send them away and have them airlocked and ejected."

"Good."

The bedroom the mechling had chosen to operate in was deserted, except for Charlotte, or assumed-to-be Charlotte. There was also the necessary medical gear keeping her healthy.

"Her eyes…" Slowly I advanced, pleased that for the moment my attraction was simmering rather than becoming stupidly elevated.

Control, yes. I could do this.

She was beautiful, for a human. "Curved splendidly," I murmured. The red dress they had her clothed in seemed free of blood, as was her face. "No bandaging?"

"Not necessary, sir. She is healing rapidly. All omegas do this. There is some research already available, sir."

I shot Quinn a look. "Omega then."

"You knew, did you not?" His front arms raised. "I see the alpha change in you."

My mouth twisted before I could stop myself. Was this distaste at being found out? "You're close to a doctor. I should have guessed you'd notice."

"Of course."

I moved nearer to the girl. "When will she wake?"

As if I pressed a switch, her eyes fluttered open. For synth eyes, these were stunningly human-looking. One was yellow and the other was violet. Human-looking apart from the precision of the structure and that bright color? "They are not as… gooey as human eyes."

"Goodness! No. I hope not. She will be able to see a pin from a thousand meters away. Gooeyness is under-rated."

"Truth." I dared to drift my hand toward her jaw—pleased at how I dwarfed her—and then to stroke along it. Softness and warmth. As my touch shifted to her cheek, her eyelashes wavered. I suppressed my desires. Not this time. This was not the time for kissing or taking. "Can you speak, female? Are you Charlotte?"

She said nothing, and the blankness in those new eyes was eerie. Was she even human anymore inside her head?

A day passed. Then another. The riots continued. The girl continued to be silent. Though she could sit up, eat, and walk a little, she didn't speak or show that she was capable of thinking.

Wherever I went, her synth eyes followed me.

I took to sitting out on the large penthouse balcony and occasionally relieving my engorgement by stroking out a climax, or two, or three. With my seat faced inward, I could watch her when Quinn helped her to shower. She couldn't stand for long by herself. Stark naked, with shower water pouring and dribbling over her, making her shiny and wet, she was as perfect as a piece of the orc-human porn I'd taken to viewing during this past year.

Always fun watching a human get reamed by giant green orc phallus… always, and especially when they were tied up and squealing.

Tradition, I had told myself the first time. Orcs and humans fucking was close to orc tradition. It was a little rude watching a guest, but, what the fuck, only I knew.

And Quinn, he knew.

Overhead rode the pseudo-sun, a pulsing pale-yellow orb, and beyond that, on the opposite side of this hollow spherical space, was where Gideon and the mauleons lived. In the seas between us were the gogogians. I had to wonder what they made of this humanoid-generated chaos. This fucking chaos.

I hated it.

Ironic, I knew. Orcs and chaos went together like axes and fighting, or cupcakes and cream.

Gogogians now, they loved dealing, buying, selling, and I had heard they somehow absorbed and enjoyed the good emotions humanoids gave them.

If they fed on our goodness, they must be starving by now.

And if the *Filthy Lucre* had been purely a starship of metal, and not a hollowed-out dragon head or asteroid—the legends and history were iffy as to which—we would have died. Houses and streets were smoldering overhead, sending smoke snaking up past the fake sun. I could smell the ashes. Black flecks floated down.

This must end. I rocked in my chair. The orcs were outnumbered by tens of thousands, and we were never good at organizing. Disorganizing, yes. Battles and making rivers of blood flow, yes, or reinforcing the missions when our smaller ships went down to planets. Wait long enough and surely the mauleons and the other humanoids would fix this?

Day three. Quinn had done as promised. Her eyes had been sent to oblivion in space and were now floating somewhere in the starry beyond. His mechling associates had also vanished. They'd walked down the sides of the tower, I was informed. I couldn't help but imagine them as perfect assassins—small, precise cutting machines. They could sever a head as easily as remove eyes.

I tapped a note of that on my comm: *Tiny assassins. Remember this.*

Smorg the sword had unleashed a lot of unknowns when he created the virus that freed the mechlings.

I was doing well, I thought. Her omega-ness had intensified, and I had withstood it. If only she would rouse and become human again.

Day four. I unfolded and rose from my balcony chair, having satisfied my most recent craving to wank. When I turned to enter the apartment, I found her just ahead and at my feet, crawling toward me.

"Fuck!" I actually jumped. "Surprise, fucking surprise." My cock swelled—of course it did. But *I* was not my cock. Not today. Not ever.

That should be my mantra: *I am not my cock.* The axe, we orcs were the axe. They can take away anything except our axes. Cocks were secondary.

I went to one knee and gently placed a hand at the side of her head, marveling at the softness of her fair hair. "Charlotte?"

Crawling was an advance on sitting.

She turned her head and licked my hand, sliding her mouth and tongue up my thumb until she reached the tip. I didn't dare to move, in case doing so made her stop. Her hand came up and she stuffed my thumb into her mouth and began to suck.

"Fuck," I croaked.

Her eyes never broke contact with mine, and with each little *wet* suck an electric shock possessed my cock.

If I didn't get away, I was doomed. I wrenched loose my hand.

She licked her mouth and her tongue slipped around the entire hole as if to gather atoms from my thumb I might have left behind. My eyes must have flared with stark desire because she flinched. I understood her. I wanted to eat her up, too. To suck on her, to fuck her into the balcony floor. It would be painful, for her.

Those atoms I imagined her sucking from my skin, was it my come? I'd cleaned up, but I smelled of it, and residue surely remained on my hand. My come had drawn her? How crazy was this omega change?

I stood and backed away. The balcony rail met my back. On hands and knees, she followed.

"More?"

Those were her first words since we rescued her.

"More?" she repeated.

I knew what she meant, but I needed control over this alpha stuff. I circled her, just out of reach, intending to go past her into the penthouse. And then what would I do? Run? In my head, I laughed at that.

An orc did not run from a succulent female who craved his cock in her. That would be stupid and cowardly.

Her hand caught at my pants. She climbed up them, clawing at my leg, and soon she was kneeling before me and reaching for where my cock dragged achingly at the rough cloth of my pants. Was there intelligence in her synth eyes? The colors intensified, the irises shrinking then ballooning out into black.

Quinn had sworn they would react to emotions the same as a flesh eye.

I grasped her hair at the back.

"If I allow you." I smirked, revealed the length of my tusks in a threatening display. "Once only."

She whimpered with need.

A primitive growl burbled from my throat as I held her, with her mouth popped open from discomfort of having her hair dragged on, or maybe it was from lust—I didn't care which. Pain and fucking. I was civilized, but the combination was irresistible to any true orc.

Rejecting our ways was easy, until a morsel like this came along.

"You are the one who should be running." I pulled out my cock and stroked myself, my fist running over those hardening spines. She watched, fascinated, following every slip and slide of my hand, up and down.

Lust was in her head, for sure. I liked being able to hypnotize a female with this.

I gripped myself harder, went slower, let my fist move treacle slow. Her breasts showed enough down the front of that shift to let me see she was breathing raggedly.

"Are you a good girl for Kragga?"

She nodded, in rhythm to the slide of my hand. I chuckled.

I screwed my other hand into her hair even tighter. I had to know. "Say your name, if you want this in your sweet, fucking mouth. The blood was roaring by then, taking over my ears, thudding by, hot and thick, same as her cunt juices would be.

I groaned at my fantasy of plunging inside her. I would never fit in this little human, untried, never reamed by any orc.

Untried. As good as virgin then? Fuck, yes.

She squeaked and her eyes dilated even more and became black pupils with a halo of violet and yellow.

"Your name? Your. Name. I'm not fucking your mouth until you show you can talk and think."

I watched that little swallow. Her tongue wet her lips then stayed out, teasing me with that soft squirmy appendage of hers. I could *feel* it wrapped around my dick.

"Char-lotte," she whispered.

"What? Louder." I leaned in, grinning at her, levering back her head, twisting the roots of her hair, making her obey.

"Charlotte!" That squeak was from pain.

I snarled, quietly.

"Good. Open wide." I reached into the loose neck of the shift and took a hold of one tit, pulled her higher using it. She squealed.

Fuck. Those squeals were addictive. I rested a finger on her front teeth, rubbed it over them, slid it on in, further, deeper, until she gagged. Then she latched on and sucked.

My cock sat up straighter, begging me to stick it there, or… My gaze drifted lower. Or between her legs.

I grunted then shoved two of my thick fingers into her mouth and my calluses caught on her soft tongue, but I stuck those fingers and in and out to wet her hole properly. "Cute little hole and so fucking perfect." I mouth fucked her a few more times, left them in deep and pressing down on her tongue. She struggled to be free.

When she reached up, I swatted away her hand before maneuvering the tip of my cock to that perfect mouth. Her synth eyes fixated on my shaft as I slowly tried to jam my dick in there.

I wasn't getting in far. I knew it. She did, too.

Not being alpha? Sure, I wasn't.

Just once. Just this once. I hip thrust and held her tightly in place with a grip on her hair to each side. She was whining and burbling. Bubbles of spit eased past where my cockhead fitted the edges of that sexy girl mouth. I couldn't get in properly, could never. Not in *this* small non-expandable hole. The other one though…

With time, training, with feeding her my come, my *basja*, I could fit. Probably.

There was ample room for my hand between that newly made knot and her lips. I wrapped it around myself, aware of the extra girth, pleased by it, feeling the erect spikes as my palm squeezed over my cock. The spikes were a good stiffness to stimulate a female, not too soft, just right. Just fucking right.

Wait until I got into her. Inside her. Spread her legs… and… all that. Words lost, I stared at her face, at the way her lips moved, and her nostrils widened, as I jerked off and pushed more dick at her, a little in, a little out.

Faster and faster, my hand moved.

I grunted.

I gulped, my temples throbbed, and I watched a row of spikes pop into her. I had made them disappear, and made her eyes open wider.

The pressure built agonizingly high. Just seeing my cock there, connecting us and inside her mouth, it was—

I groaned and released, filling her. Come poured out, erupting, as she spluttered, and it ran down her chin.

She needed to swallow it. *Basja* made females open up below.

I filled my hand with the creamy warm liquid. "Open, little bitch human."

Her mouth gaped, and I fed her, watched her swallow it down. Greedy to see that again, I scraped more off her chin and her tits and made her eat more *basja*.

"Good girl." I patted her hair with my cleanest hand, grinning. "Good Char. There. That was good."

She slumped to her knees, head down, gasping as if she, too, had come. Was this possible?

Curious, I studied her as I tucked myself into my pants, for the flushed face and the panting made me suspicious. I picked her up and placed her in a corner of the balcony, with cushions and a blanket from the balcony sofa under her. She hugged a cushion to herself and curled up.

Thinking that something might happen if I waited, I backed off and sat against the balcony glass. My breathing calmed. I hadn't even realized it needed calming.

Was Quinn still here? I could ask him what to do with a human girl I'd just made give me a blow job—a girl who seemed to awaken when I fed her come. How was this so? Not just any come, *mine*. And I'd done it while thinking I could, would, eventually take her.

I stared at the roof, two orc-heights above. Isolde meant little to me, though Gideon was a friend. He wouldn't care if I fucked this one. This dominant, knuckle-dragging alpha monster in me, was it that bad? If anything, my inner orc was waving an axe and screaming, *do this*. I grinned at that.

Grandad would have said: *Do this, you pussy-faced, pale-skinned, fool of an educated orc.*

What if I just came in her a little? Just stuck my monstrous spiky cock in her a small distance? I could thrust it in deep until she was whimpering and... *Fuck.* I shook that away.

Her knees were pulled to her chin, and Char stared at me from her corner.

Char. Much better than Charlotte. It meant to burn. I inhaled. My nostril hairs were singeing just fantasizing about her in my bed or chained beside it, and forever available.

With every minute that eased by, more alertness came to those pretty eyes.

That blue shift she wore, it should go. How could I admire this catch of mine, if she was dressed in something that hid her body?

Except I shouldn't be doing this. Should I? My resolve not to go alpha had cracked.

Her legs were coyly tucked beneath her, but I remembered them, and that ass waggling as she crawled to me. Would orc *basja* help make her take big orc dick? Normal *basja* did, but my come might be different. Alpha-omega sex was unknown territory.

Mauleon come had worked on Isolde. She had swallowed Gideon's full length. His boast had been loud and proud.

"Tell me about what happened on that ship. On Vedrock's ship, the *Social Deviance*." A complicated question, but I wanted to test her.

Had she lost much of her brain power, somehow?

"I..."

Ahhh, she spoke.

And she stopped.

I frowned and jerked my chin, indicating to continue. Her focus shifted to past my shoulder, and I thought she looked toward Rishnak, at the partially ruined towers, with their haphazard outlines. Some parts had fallen, while others were like this one, and mostly intact.

A small crease formed on her brow above her nose.

"How are your eyes, Char?" I asked.

"The fires, what are they?"

5

CHAR (lotte)

"Char?"

"Your name is Char now, girl. Answer me. Are your eyes good?"

Good?

I stared at him for a very long time, long enough for the fires to be etched onto my eyeballs, even though those flames ranged across the sky, somehow, above his head. Confused, I switched from those distant infernos, to him, and back, several times.

Was this a starship, or not? I'd seen enough sci-fi movies to know that this place was too big, too untidy, too not-metal to be one. There weren't enough doors that went *whoosh* when they opened, and how could something with this much wasted space be a ship? Traveling across the stars required more panache.

Also, fires on a ship? It would explode.

"Where are we? Really?"

The orc creature frowned, and his large green brows met like squishy corrugated iron. All of him was rough, rugged, and mildly green. He would outweigh a bull, and maybe out fight one, too. His hands had fingers the size of sausages—which was something I recalled intimately, from sucking on them. The warmth of a blush flooded my cheeks.

Had that truly been me? The memory was hazy, but he'd asked a question while I was being mortified and was waiting patiently for an answer.

Patience was not something I expected in an orc.

His voice sounded threatening and rough—as if he gargled rocks once a day, for fun.

"Why do you ask about my eyes?" I touched beneath one, and memories rocked me.

I'd gone blind. The man who had carried me from the *Social Deviance* had mentioned blood in my eyes. "You healed me?"

"We did. In a way. I'm glad you can see."

"So am I." Thank fuck. Something to be grateful for. I should say thank you, shouldn't I?

The spikes protruding from one biceps, the fierceness in his gaze, and the metal rings and violent hairstyle told me an adamant *no, do not dare to thank him.*

He'd already made me give him a blow job, except I, too, recalled my fierce craving. Had I orgasmed during that? *Fuckness, I had.* The slickness between my thighs was late testimony to that fact.

"We replaced them. The doc said we had to. Your eyes were poisoning you. Those are synth eyes."

A ringing turned up in my ears, and I lowered my head and clutched it, felt myself grow dizzy. The balcony was spinning, tilting. "What did you say?" I whispered.

A rasp of clothes and boots, then his smell, those warned me he drew near.

His hand was laid on my back. "Are you okay?"

This orc who had removed my eyes asked that. Confused and scared, I growled at him. "Get away from me."

"What?"

At least the anger had nuked the dizziness. I spat next to the boot I found beside me, growled again. Don't curse him, fool. "Please, go away!"

I heard him straighten, saw his shadow leave me.

"Hmmm. Should spank that out of you? Punish you? I would, but it might jar loose your eyes?" Was that a snicker?

Evil of him, to be amused at his dark joke.

"Fuck!" It was a fuck tinted with despair and agony, but… I blinked away a sudden attack of tears. I had new eyes. They worked. Not long ago, they had not worked, and I'd been ready to end it all. Though how long had it been since I left the *Social Deviance*? The main thing was, I could see.

I peeked past my fingers and watched the fires dim and brighten. I could see.

I should be grateful for that.

"Is this truly a starship?"

"Of course it is. You're on the *Filthy Lucre*. Why did you spit?" He snorted. "I could crush you with one finger, and you spit."

He could. His bare green chest was decorated with black tattoos. They wound over his body, across edges and into hollows, mapping the shape of him. The ridges of his muscles were over-written with ink, and that only made him appear ever more fearsome.

Even so, I hated why I was here—abducted along with Isolde and others from Earth. Why should I ever thank him? My eyes, my weird new omega power, none of that would have happened if these alien assholes had not taken us.

"I spat because you tasted awful. I would do it again, too." Yet I said that to his feet, not daring to meet those yellow eyes.

He laughed quietly and stretched, making his body crack and pop and his leather harness creak. Then he walked away to lean his side against the balcony.

"My come brought you back to life. Don't mock the good stuff."

"Say what?"

"You heard me. You were near death and then smelled my come and came crawling to me."

"*Ewww*." Had I really? A memory poked at me: of grit under my hands and knees and a croaky *please*, of a hand held toward a fuzzy figure of a man who was not a man. "Shit," I whispered.

"You spit and growl like cornered prey. So, your eyes work, this is good. Now thank me for rescuing you. You would have died on the dockyards."

I considered his words. They sounded true, and I wasn't surprised.

What I'd done had unleashed something terrible upon the universe. It had distorted reality. I might have hallucinated that. *Might*, but knew I had not. My certainty was rooted deep in my bones.

Oh, yes.

I gasped as colors blurred and everything stretched then snapped back into place.

My omega-gifted senses had reawakened with a strange, surreal twist of the air itself and my guts.

Even now, here on this balcony, where I was unsure of what and where anything else was located, I could feel the starship engines beneath me, rumbling and flaring. They mangled space to wrench this ship from one part of the heavens to another. It was why the singularities had ripped the fabric of the universe. Why we omegas had been made and the alphas, too.

It was why this orc was an alpha.

I need not have asked him if this was a starship, for I was connected intimately to her power. I could feel the tumultuous energies as easily as I felt my own pulse.

This was nothing like before, not as strong a connection. Still, it was there, beneath my butt, if not at my fingertips.

"Hello," I said softly, to the starship.

"You asked about the fires." The orc pulled me back into the world around me.

"Yes, I did." I raised my head and this time I looked into his eyes. I frowned. A metal ring pierced through one shaggy eyebrow, and it bothered me. The ring made me look more closely at his face. Ugly? Yes. But also as horribly compelling as his body.

My omega responded to his maleness like a pet to a long-lost owner. I sighed.

It was an uncontrollable reaction, yet where was my identity when I grew wet merely from glancing at his damnable face? I shuddered as my pussy clamped in, and I breathed as slowly as I could through parted lips. Any worse and I would beg to be fucked. Heat shimmied up through my body, and my nipples poked at the loose cloth. The slightest brush of fabric made me grit my teeth.

I shifted my legs under me, trying to evade this arousal.

My next words were shaky. "What is your name?"

"Kragga."

Figured. Even his name was a rocky avalanche of syllables.

A smile teased those heavy lips, as if he knew my thoughts and saw my arousal. He was alpha, so it was entirely possible.

"I lead the black orcs. There are also red orcs and green orcs. It has to do with the color of our tattoos."

"I will call you Kragga then." I nodded. Be polite, I reminded myself, for self-preservation purposes, so as not to get turned into jam. "But you have to call me Charlotte. I'm not Char."

He grinned, revealing his ivory-colored tusks in great detail. "You are Char because I say you are. Easier to say, to spell, and—"

My scowl made him pause.

"Also, it's Char because you're mine. Currently." He drawled the last word as if it were an afterthought.

"I'm not anyone's." I said it plaintively, but one could hope.

"You are. You only exist here as a possession. Isolde has personhood, but you? You're not Vedrock's anymore, so you're mine, unless someone else claims you."

"I was *never* Vedrock's." He'd left me alone, even though a tenuous alpha-omega link had played at my mind, and surely at his? "You mentioned Isolde. You know her?" Please, please know her. "Is she okay? Can I see her?"

He shot me an assessing stare. "Meeting Isolde is difficult. She's fine and has a mate, a mauleon called Gideon. You were Vedrock's. According to Grut, you were his. We found the records. There are rumors about what happened on that ship."

He'd glossed over taking me to Isolde as if it were impossible.

"Some think he had something to do with the alpha omega abnormality. What happened on the *Social Deviance*?"

That question chilled me. If I spoke the whole truth, I would condemn myself.

"I don't know." A simple answer, for it meant I had less chance of tripping myself. I knew. I knew entirely too much about my own actions, if not what Vedrock had done before I arrived.

"Are you sure?" He scanned my face. "What made your eyes go bad and fill with blood and poison?"

"I was tortured. He saw I was omega and wanted me to do *ummm* something."

Truth. He had beaten me. He had wanted me to use my omega powers, but I had pre-empted him and he had never figured out what I was capable of.

Suspicion rode Kragga's face. "Something?"

Hurriedly I added, "Vedrock thinks omegas have weird powers that come to them."

"And do you? Gideon said Isolde saw visions of the future."

"Maybe some of us." I flattened my mouth. "Not all of us, obviously."

"Not you?"

I shook my head.

"You're lying, and you know you are."

"No." I swallowed. "I am not." What would he do?

This was a stand-off. Or would he start pulling out my entrails to make me talk? That would work. Vedrock had seemed to be willing to do anything except permanently hurt his omegas.

"Do you remember not being able to talk? For days you didn't seem aware of anything."

Unfortunately, I remembered crawling to him.

"Think long and hard," he said. "Very long and very hard. It may remind you of sucking on my cock and licking come off my hand."

I glared. Trust me to find a guy with an awful sense of humor in the middle of this mess. A guy? Whyever did I think that? He was so *not* a guy.

The doorbell rang and interrupted his grin.

Saved by an actual doorbell, in orc territory. I had never forgotten the orc hordes in *Lord of the Rings*. We were in an apartment in some sort of skyscraper. This seemed the equivalent of that train that went to a halfway, nonexistent platform in Harry Potter.

"In!" he bellowed.

A door opened and shut. "It's me."

"Vagrax! Come to the balcony."

A second, slimmer orc arrived, though he was still broad enough to challenge doorways. This one had long, coarse black hair that hung past his shoulders, though some of it was caught in sticks and rings, to make it project upward on top of his head. Grass growing on a manure heap was more fashionable than this.

He eyed me. "What did you do with her? She looks better."

"Mouth fuck. Only. So far. My come works wonders."

The orc's brows rose high.

Shocked by that blatant admission, I stayed curled in the corner, with my hands grasping the blanket as if it could protect me.

"She's lying about something… What are you here for Vagrax?"

"Dinner. Urgel caught a few big veelers in the tunnels, and we're spit roasting them." He licked his tusk. "We could do that to her if you bring her."

"Spitroast her?" Kragga actually sounded curious.

"Yes."

"What? No!" I shrank into the wall.

"She asks 'what'. *Hur hur*." Vagrax leered.

"You cut out my eyes! You made me drink your come to revive me, which is just the worst fucking cure ever! I was… I was in a coma, or so you said, and now you threaten to do that!" I had dropped the blanket to gesture wildly.

I was being stupid, but my head was going to explode.

If they killed me and spit-roasted me, or the reverse order, it would serve me right.

"He cut out your eyes?" Vagrax gasped melodramatically.

"She has perfectly good new ones the mechlings implanted."

"But first they used those sharp little cutting tools that go *scree-whirr* to remove the old ones? Blood flew? Why did you not invite me, Kragga?"

Again, I glared. What the fuck was it with these orcs?

"Shut up. He jokes." Kragga slammed Vagrax across the back in what must be a friendly blow then shook him by the neck. The other orc barely noticed. "Your eyes work. This is normal here, if not on your Earth. Though not to have the mechlings do it in a bedroom, I admit."

Now he said this? My mouth was open. I shut it. My eyes had been cut out. I wasn't sure I would ever get over that, when I thought about it.

Stop thinking it.

"A banquet then. A feast. Yes, we will go. Her, too. She has synth eyes, so Vagrax, shield your ass or she will see up it to your last dinner."

"Gross," I muttered. These eyes seemed no different in sight than any human eyes. Unless I counted the soft *shshh* they made now and then.

I was going to be taken to an orc banquet. I had synthetic eyes. I was alive. And I had recently fucked up the universe and could not tell anyone for fear of being ended.

Or would they ask me to reverse the process if they believed what I said? Maybe.

I couldn't do that. This was how things were from now on.

"Kragga, you need to decide what she is. Do you claim her as captive, or is this girl to be given to others?"

"I will not gift her to others."

They'd dropped into seriousness. I wasn't sure I preferred this to bad jokes.

"Claim her as your captive then, or you'll have challenges. A *jus-rak* ceremony is needed tonight."

"Challenges and fights, now, would be bad. You are right. It's required and tradition." He sighed. "I will claim her then."

Openmouthed, I looked at these two calmly discussing my fate. "Just take me to Isolde, please?"

"She cannot help you," Vagrax said grimly. "We cannot reach the mauleons anymore. We used the last fuel for the ax-ramblers to rescue you. Those could do fast jumps across the middle of the core, bypassing the sun. Now?" He made a vexed face. "We'd have to surface walk. Between us and them is the sea, and where the riots and fighting rage."

"Or the deeper tunnels," Kragga pointed out. "We could use those, but it would take days, and many orcs would die. We will wait for direction."

Direction? Who was there to do directing?

"Take action," I urged, standing and propping myself against the wall. "It's just your starship out there. You told me this."

"We wait," Kragga repeated. "There is no other choice, and I will claim you, even if the idea repulses me."

"Repulses?" Vagrax sounded puzzled. "Okay, why? She's a beauty, for a human. Lush and a good mouthful, everywhere."

"I'm not a hamburger," I grumbled.

They ignored me.

"Being too alpha will worry my black orcs and worries me. It is tradition to claim an unclaimed captured female, but it also looks alpha." He rubbed his chin then stepped nearer.

I squished further backward into the wall.

Kragga's smile hardened. "Take off the shift. We must judge your body. You cannot wear that rag to an orc *jus-rak* ceremony."

He took one more step. The background rumble of his breathing was unnerving. It must sound like this when a lion leaned over a dragged-down zebra and prepared to eat it. To keep my eyes on his I had to tilt my head back a long way, exposing my throat, and I knew I was making myself vulnerable. My rising arousal and shaky legs were testimony to my conflicted emotions.

Being towered over by this evil-eyed creature with hot, smelly breath should not be turning me on.

Slowly he reached out and nestled the *V* of his hand over my neck, then he pressed that hand down until, whenever I swallowed, I must register the roughness of his skin on my throat.

I closed my eyes, drew a breath, opened them.

"Now, girl. Lie again, and you go to the banquet naked. Finding clothes for humans is a pain in the orc ass in Rishnak. What do you know about what happened on the *Social Deviance*?"

"Nothing?" I squeaked.

"Why..." He dipped his head, and his mouth was at my ear, lips rasping over the lobe when he spoke. "I hoped you'd say that."

"Bastard," I whispered.

He bit my neck, his tusks digging in, and I only half-suppressed my squeal at the pain. And the delayed thrill that ran straight to my clit? That troubled me.

"I'm sure that was not an insult."

"Liar," I whispered, unsure why I was almost daring him to punish me.

"The things I should do to you, but they can wait until the banquet." He straightened but kept his hand in place. "It is customary for another orc to dress the female. Your job, Vagrax. No molesting her."

"Done. How do you want this to be?"

He studied my face then dragged up the shift, to expose my breasts and below. My pussy leaked more wetness, and I kept my legs closed to hide it. "Mostly naked. Nothing painful, yet. I suppose I must use the *jus-rak* chest my parents and tribe gifted me when I first went off-planet."

Vagrax grunted. "Yours is unused? You've not cracked open the chest? After all this—"

"Shush. Yes. Unused." His mouth quirked at one end. "Collar, leash, the chain garment, and whatever else seems to suit her. Bring the rest. I will wait for you to dress her, and we will leave as one." He squeezed his hand onto my neck. "Do not give him strife. You have permission to whip her ass if she does anything wrong, Vagrax."

"And I vow to use your permission with great joy."

"If," he said, looking aside, his eyes hard. "She disobeys you. Do not overstep."

I didn't say anything more. The atmosphere had shifted. I didn't like this, not one iota, but I obeyed when Vagrax took me into a large room bedecked with enough weapons on the wall to outfit a small army—rifles of some sort, wicked pistols with blades, axes, and then more axes.

He opened a red, carved timber chest and tut-tutted.

"Let us begin. Take off all your clothes, girl."

I preferred *Char* to girl.

I pulled off the shift and stripped off my panties. No bra had been given to me, so there I stood, naked with this orc circling me, and my arms wrapped over myself.

"Nice. The chains are a good choice. They will adjust to your small size, as will the collar. What a pity I cannot clip something to your tits." Merriment danced in his eyes, and I had to refrain from a rude retort.

Kink had been my favorite hobby on Earth, a part of my life, really. Here though, with orcs doing whatever they pleased? There was great danger, and there was fear.

It was an inexplicable fear, for had I not recently tried to, sort-of, do bad things to the universe?

I'd intended a back-handed revenge on Vedrock, but I may as well have tried to nuke everything, and I still wasn't sure what I had accomplished. Fear did not respect my past suicidal impulses. One careless slap from an orc and I would have multiple fractures.

Slim silvery chains were laced about my body, like a never-there dress. A spray of chains cradled my breasts. A gathering of three thicker strands slipped between my legs where they nestled into the divide between my swollen lower lips. I tried to remain unconcerned that one chain was not only swimming in my juices but also rubbing over my clit whenever I moved in any direction. From the main waist chain, several others tinkled in a pretend skirt that reached to just below my mons. Absolutely nothing of me was concealed.

Even Gaultier might be appalled. Orcs probably thought fashion was heresy.

"Last is this." Triumphantly, he held up a black collar with stubby spikes dotting the entire length.

Do you have one of those in pink, with diamonds, stalled on my tongue.

With it buckled on my neck, and he was gentle as he did so, and with a chain leash connected, I was dropped into memories of myself on Earth at the club.

Yet Kragga was so un-Earthlike, with his tusks, greenish skin, and immense tattooed body. Battle scars as well as tattoos crisscrossed his bare chest.

This wasn't Earth. These were not men, and no matter their flair for awful jokes, they were never going to be safe to be around—especially not when I was only a possession.

6

KRAGGA

Someone took an axe to my breathing when she stepped into the hallway beside Vagrax.

I almost choked on my tongue.

The orc held her leash and a rolled bundle of gear from my *jus-rak* chest. I could smell her arousal, which only made this weirder. We were not bonded. I was not in rut. It had to be the alpha orc in me lusting after her.

Being alpha had advantages I could grow to appreciate. I inhaled again through my nose, letting her pheromones percolate down.

With each stride she took, her hips swayed, and the chains fastened about them tinkled and swept from side to side in a wave. Her ruby-red mouth... My cock surely lengthened by a fist merely at the sight of it. My gaze cruised and skipped, lower, across, pausing here and there at nipples and navel before continuing down her body, until I came to the slim arrow of hair pointing to her pussy.

The chains about her breasts had me aching to do what I had forbidden to Vagrax.

"Fuck," I murmured.

"Yes." Vagrax smirked. "See, you needed this. Not using that chest full of good stuff was criminal."

"Hmmm." I took the end of the leash from him, looped it around her neck, once, twice, and pulled her slowly toward me. "Are you going to behave for me at this *jus-rak* ceremony? To kneel when I say, spread your legs on command?" A flush rose visibly on her face, neck, and breasts. "Suck my cock if told to?"

"No!" She tried to step away, although the feverish glaze in her eyes said she was lying.

I held her still. "Why the soft rasp of arousal in your voice?" I curled her lower lip with one finger.

She only blinked at me.

"You lie badly. I look forward to striping your rear end. Come."

Despite her protests, she was silent in the elevator, trapped as she was between me and Vagrax.

The banquet was in our usual eating area—an old room large enough for fifty black orcs and with a see-through arched ceiling high above. The glass-like material was cracked and marked by the ages and by smoke, but it remained intact. There were no trees above to fall and break the glass, nothing but the fake sun during the day and the fake moon it transformed into at night. On the opposite side of the core, the radiance from fires shone brighter than the moon. They seemed lesser than before. Perhaps little remained to burn?

My throne had been prepared, and I sat there, legs spread widely to show my dominance. It was my right with every meal, but I rarely bothered. For the *jus-rak*, whoever asserted the claim was allowed to be seated on this black, padded chair with the armrests of gold-and-black serpents, the frame of axes and spears, and the skull of some weird forgotten creature with sharp red teeth perched atop the back.

It was a little over the top in menace, but I liked it.

"Chain her there." I pointed to the cube of stone before my throne.

To either side, tables ran down the length of the room to the double-doored entrance, opposite. The other orcs were mostly seated and greedily watching the display of my captive, as Vagrax walked Char down the cleared middle toward me.

A fireplace lay far to the left, with three orc-sized veelers propped over the flames on revolving spits. The fireplace wasn't an original feature, but at some time in the previous hundred years, a few enterprising orcs had knocked a hole in the wall to build it. The cracks running down the wall above it were probably an omen. If it collapsed, we would move to a new tower.

For this parade, I'd given the leash to Vagrax and instructed him to, "Chain her loosely at wrists and ankles then leave her."

The cube had several thick steel anchor points designed for this.

Her eyes were wide, and she was warily observing the orcs as she padded past them, even though they leered at her nakedness. Yet she did not seem too fearful. Instead, she glanced in my direction, boldly riding her eyes up my body, as if I calmed her by being present. If she knew my perverted thoughts, would she be more afraid, or less?

Vagrax placed her on the top of the waist-high cube then locked the manacles to her so that her ankles were far apart. The wrist chains were left longer. She could sit there with her legs apart or go to her hands and knees, but every shift of her body sent the long chains rattling and sliding over stone, over flesh. Every shift of her body brought eyes to her.

She could not conceal what lay between her legs.

I shifted on the throne, aware of my erection pulsing in anticipation. Fucking her here was not possible, not exactly. *Jus-rak* I reminded myself, was only the beginning.

"Nice ass!" someone yelled.

"Do we fuck her by numbers or by the alphabet, Kragga?" another taunted.

It was customary to heckle whoever claimed her. It was also customary to share the captive, a little, to let the others use the training dildos on her, or a spreader device, and sometimes to finger or tongue her while this was done.

First, we would eat.

I waved my hand to get them to lower the volume of their voices, then rose to my feet and bellowed, "We begin the *jus-rak* feast, my brother orcs! Eat, drink, and feast your orcish eyes upon my beautiful captive Charlotte, now to be known as Char."

"You will never fit that large cock of yours in her," Mog yelled back. "I vow to help you with that small hole of hers when the eating is done! As do all our brother orcs!" He opened his arms to include everyone.

I hesitated only a few heartbeats then added, more quietly, "Yes. It shall be so, brother orcs."

A roar shook the room as fifty orcs banged on the table and raised mugs and flagons, but I was watching Char, crouched upon the cube. My smile had weakened.

More and more the inclination was rising to forbid other orcs to touch her. One did not have to allow it. But if I did not, they would say the alpha had me.

Which was the wisest? Which could I bear to do?

The unrolled bundle of my *jus-rak* gear lay to my right, on an identical cube of stone.

The spreaders, too. Two had wildly devious jaws to part her labia, along with a tube for insertion that split and widened upon cranking. Again, I shifted on the throne, only gripping and squeezing my cock once.

The various-sized dildos ranged from small to extra-large. I had not yet assessed the insides of her cunt to see what to begin with.

The black orcs were stuffing their faces and gulping down beer. My own platter and flagon sat untended beside the gear. Twice, I rallied and took morsels to her on a fork, as well as a goblet of wine. There was a strange relief in seeing the fire in her eyes when her fingers brushed mine, or when, once, I brushed my lips over her lips and then delicately over her shoulder. It would not do to have her be mortally afraid.

What else was in that gift from my family and tribe? I left the throne and went to look. A decade ago, I'd gone off-planet in search of a dream, of being more than an orc with an axe, and this gift had been left unexamined and neglected.

The tube of cream that contained a drug to relax and dilate a female, I nudged off the stone. It was expired. Only a fool would use it when my own come had already done wondrous things to her.

On hands and knees, Char followed what I did, with a little crease of worry between her eyes—her yellow and violet eyes. The orcs at the table beyond her were clearly getting a fine view of her pussy. I grimaced but ignored them. Smacking anyone tonight would be rude, no matter how harsh my annoyance… make that my anger. It crushed that anger.

I would not follow the way of other alphas.

I showed my tusks. Two of the three orcs went hurriedly back to their meals.

I gathered the two shiny clamps lurking among the gear and strolled to her, watched her sit back with her legs askew beneath. "You look both fuckable and as if I should enshrine you, somehow, gilded and forever nude with your cunt on display."

"*Ummm*. That would be a no?"

Did she believe I might do it? Perhaps. She must have a poor opinion of the morality of orcs. We did tend to rape, pillage, and destroy when commanded to do so. Or sometimes when not.

"Only teasing you." Then I leaned further, took her face in hand, and kissed her.

When she was gasping beneath my lips and tusks, I slid my free hand down her neck, awed by the soft smoothness, until I found her breast. The kissing became hot, wet, and lazy, as our tongues met and played. She dared to lick over one tusk then suck on it. So, I turned my head to fuck her mouth with my tongue and hold her locked beneath me.

She tasted of wine and desire.

Breath on breath, with her eyes on mine, I felt her stiffening nipples brush my chest and then my searching palm.

"Mine." I squashed one between finger and thumb, and her lips slackened and parted. A gasp of pleasure or pain escaped her.

"I eat your little noises with joy." And I ran more bites and kisses down the side of her neck.

Blindly, I had fished a clamp from where I'd left them on the stone. I ducked my head and sucked hard on her breast then opened the jaws of the clamp and slowly closed them on that pert, wet nipple.

I let go.

When I straightened, she was staring at where the clamp perched on her, squeezing flat that delicate human flesh.

"Ohmigod," she said quietly. "Oh. Ffff…uck."

"It hurts but feels good?"

Her reply was a shaky "*Unh*" sound. I took it to mean yes and repeated my actions on the other nipple. She squealed and tried to clutch my arm, but the shortness of the chain attaching her wrist to the stone jerked her to a halt.

I backed further away, my eyes surely gleaming with sadistic mischief. Her clit was visibly erect. What a perfect girl for an orc—she liked pain.

That was worth it. So very worth it. How could I stomach food when I had this female before me?

Her breasts had my clamps jutting from them, and every wobble of that precious flesh of hers made me ache even more. She seemed enraptured and was studying them, with her eyes closing and opening.

Why leave the widening of her and the training to my brother black orcs? This female should be mine alone. She *was* mine.

I had an idea. One that would please them, and I went back to the gear and selected a middle-sized dildo. Lubricant? I eyed between her legs and saw the shine of her juices on her thighs. As I watched, a glistening string fell to the stone from her pussy.

No lubricant needed.

"Do you need me to fuck you, tonight, little Char?"

What would she say?

I reached around behind her to slide my palm over the expanse of her ass then downward, searching past her rear hole and along between her legs. Her cleft was engorged and slippery.

She pressed her face into the angle of my neck and shoulder, and her breathing turned ragged.

"Are you trying to hide your reaction? One?" I slipped a finger into her entrance and found little resistance, though thrusting further brought a groan from her, then a shudder, as her walls spasmed onto my finger.

"You are ready for me. If only I was a small human." I smiled, enjoying the heated pulse and squash of her flesh on mine. "Two?"

I pushed a second in to join the first, fucking her until I could go no further inside.

This female had been fucked before. It would be easier for her than for a true virgin.

"Three?" I removed the two and tried three. The wet squelch as they were pushed in and out, the pungent scent of her omega state, it stirred my blood like nothing ever had before.

I could barely hear past the thunder of my heart.

I pulled out of her and stepped away, staggering a little before I recovered.

The tables had fallen silent. My orcs seemed mesmerized.

I waved my wet hand.

They laughed, cheered, then drank a toast to me.

Or maybe it was to her. She sat crouched over, with her head lowered, and she was clearly dazed. This from only fingers? My cock would be a fucking revelation to her.

Not an idle male boast, for once.

The control I had over her excitement, her lust, it was enough to wipe from my mind any thoughts of not being alpha to her omega.

I wiped across my mouth with the back of my hand, bumping past my tusks as I considered this. I needed to show my brother orcs some generosity or they would become resentful, and think me weak and unable to rein in my alpha.

"I will allow this following act!" I declared. "Vagrax and two others can use this dildo on her, and you can try to make her come." I grinned. "Succeed and we can put something in her little asshole. But after that, only I will touch her! Vagrax will choose the winners!"

Then I retreated to my throne to watch them choose.

At last, Vagrax and other two orcs stepped forth.

Vagrax, Urzul, and Lagakh approached Char where she waited, clamped and already aroused. Could I, would I, stay away from her if she came close to climax?

Her panting had lessened, and she watched the three orcs advance then whimpered to me, "No. Please?" She appealed with those big, swimming synth eyes. My heart hurt. I considered intervening. I must not. I satisfied myself by noting how nicely sadistic this was—to make her accept and take this.

She pleaded again.

"It is our way. You will do this." Then I added, mangling a phrase I had learned from Earth movies, "Sorry, but it's a no. Denial is a bitch."

Her whimpering intensified as the others surrounded her, until

Vagrax grabbed a handful of her hair, and pushed her into a proper all-fours position with her ass upward. "Begin."

Urzul brandished the dildo like a sword then lowered it and aimed.

At the first touch of it on her cunt, she focused on the surface of the stone. The only thing she was contemplating was where that dildo was going. I knew where it was going—inside her, as far inside as it would fit, and medium to an orc was huge for a human.

I gripped my cock through my pants and began to stroke myself. The *basja* I had already fed her would help, but feeding more to her, soon, was a must. An emergency, even?

I smiled grimly as she made an *O* with her mouth that widened as they screwed that thing into her.

She faced me, with the clamps dangling from her nipples and her breasts jerking in time with the force they applied to the dildo and her pussy. I could only guess the depth being achieved.

When she began to pant, I rose from the throne and went to her, slipping my thumb into her mouth for her to suck and moan upon. Being this near to an omega in this state was agonizing.

This close to my omega.

She stiffened and shut her eyes, unmistakably about to orgasm. I removed my thumb and kissed her, open-mouthed, to absorb her little cries, to feel her quivers through my lips. Without looking, I found a clamp and drew it downward, stretching her nipple while I kept her trapped. We locked eyes, and I observed every flutter of her eyelashes, every facial movement, every shudder and frown as she wondered if what she was about to do was something that irrevocably bound us together. *It was. Oh, it was.*

Our lips brushed against the other as I spoke. "My brother orcs may stimulate you to climax, but it is I who commanded this, and only I who will keep you and own you."

Then she whined into my mouth and jerked into a full-on spluttering, gasping climax, with her fingers clawed into my bare chest as if she intended to rip a piece of me loose.

7

CHAR

Slumped onto my forearms and forehead, I recovered while the orcs talked and extracted what they had fed into me. In my heavy-breathing, mind-blown world, they barely existed. They were distant voices and hands I could not see. Kragga was before me, acknowledging my desires, combing my hair with his big fingers. Was it his unexpected sadism that had felled me. I knew this and dreaded it happening again. It was somehow wrong to react to an orc in that way?

Even now, he kissed the side of my mouth, my ear. He pulled me higher to bestow my upper breasts with kisses and nibbles, while I panted. Then he suddenly unclamped my nipples.

Both of them. Swiftly. That fucking *hurt*.

"Fuck! Ow, ow, ow." I tried to clutch my breasts but tangled the chains under my knees. It was too much effort to scream.

I moaned as he massaged my nipples between his coarse and scratchy finger and thumb. His touch was nirvana, inexplicably melting the hurts.

"The moon and sun above could not surpass the beauty of your unhinged lusts."

For a pulsing second, I wondered if I was hearing what was not there.

No, the orc, Kragga, had said that. I did not raise my head from where I rested my forehead on the ungiving stone.

"Shakespeare?" I whispered.

"No, I don't know them. Just me."

What the fuck?

"You've missed your calling, sir."

"I get a sir from you?"

"Temporarily." I actually smiled at that. "Also, I think..." I sucked in a few breaths before I mumbled, "You dropped your orc card, with those words."

I wasn't sure where this was going, considering I had just been fucked by a dildo whose size had frightened years off my life. Even I wasn't sure how far it had entered me.

"You promised more if she came," someone said. "Her asshole."

Oh shite.

"I did." Kragga sounded dubious and annoyed.

Alarmed, I propped myself higher on my palms. I'd missed hearing that promise being made. I shot Kragga a pleading look, and he shrugged.

Annoyed, yes. Willing to help me, no. Since I was still chained to the stone, there was little I could do to escape them.

Orc two—I had named them with numbers—sauntered to the kink equipment Vagrax had brought, and he selected another dildo. This one was black, and it had probably been designed for elephants. *That* in my ass?

I shrank backward as far as possible as the three returned to me. "Uh-uh." Vigorously, I shook my head. "Noooo."

And that was when, to put it mildly, all hell broke loose.

A blue tentacle roped into the room through a high window to the right, sending shattered glass whirring through the air while shards crashed down and spun over the floor. It wrapped an orc in its grasp, tossed him high, and smashed him down again. A metal sign landed on the poor orc, and with a clatter it tumbled to the floor. The tentacle sucked back through the window and was gone. The passage of the creature outside was betrayed by the sounds of things breaking, some screams and shouts, and then all the noises of mayhem lessened, as if whatever it was had wandered away down the street.

"Right. Get weapons and three armed orcs get out there ASAP to see what that was!" Kragga bellowed as he unlocked the cuffs on my wrists and ankles at maniacal speed. "Done. You get yourself upstairs. Can I trust you to? If you don't, *that* may get you." His heavy brow wrinkled.

I nodded and slid off the stone cube, disorientated and afraid.

"Good." He eyed me a moment longer. "You should have an escort but..." He ripped his gaze down me, down my utterly naked body, if one excluded chains from being called clothing, and he huffed. The orc huffed and looked disconcerted. "Fuck. I can't trust any orc to take you. Get! Upstairs. Wait. Clothes, clothes..."

A scream from outside made him decide to chase after the rest of the orcs.

Had he forgotten that I had no idea what number his room was or even the floor? The tentacle action had blanked his brain. Also, tentacles that size? While the orcs ran out the front door in one direction, whooping, screaming, and brandishing various axes and spears, rifles, and small guns, I ran out the door but in the opposite direction. Toward the elevators, yes, then past them.

While the orcs are away, the girl will put as much distance as possible between her and them. Orgasms were never reason enough to stay with an abusive, *ummm*, whatever he was.

Was he abusive, though? I kept jogging while I questioned my own motives. Being barefoot, I should take care where I stepped.

No time for philosophy. Kragga might notice I was missing at any moment, and I was in orc territory.

How did I get to where Isolde now lived? On the other side of the core, he'd said.

And their vehicles were out of fuel—though that could be a lie to stop me from trying to leave?

Naked and unwilling to stop long enough to search cupboards—not that there were any, I found an exit and opened a door that led into a stairwell. There was light here, though only a few of the light units functioned. The stairs must be emergency ones, and these went both up and down.

Any vehicles would be kept in a garage. Did orcs have garages? According to *LOTR* they had nose rings and spears and an awful choice in masters every single time. Why go to the guy with the evil, all-seeing eye when the other people had beer, green valleys, parties with fireworks, and sunshine?

Hurriedly, I made the wise choice to descend, to find this legendary ax-rambler and try to start its engines. I prayed no tentacle monsters were waiting for me. Or that it preferred the taste of orc. I sprinted down the stairs, only to find they ended one flight down and the door was askew, knocked off its hinges.

The light flickered and showed enough of what was out the door to make my stomach sink. The vehicles out there had been crushed by falling ceilings and concrete long ago. Only rust and some sort of rats that squeaked, remained. The squeaks grew louder and more numerous. Red eyes glowed in the dimness.

"Fuck."

I ran back up the stairs, ignoring the door I had used before. There were voices and tramping boots? The orcs might be returning.

Quietly, I ascended. On the ninth floor up, I discovered another door I could open, and I stepped out onto a rooftop. By then I was exhausted and limping.

I hobbled out under the fake, bluish moon and discovered this was probably a secondary tower. The one I'd been in before was higher, and this roof was some sort of landing pad. Vehicles were here. Three of them. There was no exit, no road leading down, so whatever those rectangular shapes with wheels might be, they could surely fly. Without wings, yes, but this was an alien starship with alien tech.

I went closer, more aware of my nudity here, beneath the moon, and open to the observation of anyone gazing out the windows of any of the four or five towers that overlooked this rooftop.

The vehicle was mostly black, had skinny metal fins on the roof, and red graffiti all over it—rudimentary red skulls, crossed axes, and sketched X marks that might be a scoreboard of enemy killed. Or pizza scores. Who knew? Not me.

A wind skittered across the exposed area, which made me wonder how this interior core of a starship could have anything resembling weather. Could it rain, as well?

I pulled open the door of the driver's cabin and hauled myself up and inside. It took some effort from my fatigued legs due to the height of this thing. The seats inside were enormous. They were made for orcs, of course.

Starter switch?

The crab translator embedded below my nape deciphered the writing, and the dashboard labels resolved into words. In the blue of the moonlight, with my forefinger I traced the main one emblazoned across the black plastic-like substance of the dash.

"Ax-rambler. Model FC18," I murmured. "What if you do have enough fuel? Dare I try to fly you out of here?" I peered up through the slanted windshield at the moon. Up there, somewhere, was Isolde.

Dare I?

I found the fuel gauge, conveniently labelled FUEL, but the arrow was on empty.

Maybe it only worked when switched on?

Maybe that was so, but no matter how long I searched, I could not find an ignition or a place for a key, or even a button that said START HERE.

"Fuck." I let my head tilt backward, and I lay there, soaking up the deceptive peace.

Would they find me if I stayed still? Probably. Where could I go? Nowhere.

I closed my eyes and rested a few minutes then sighed, exited, and closed the door quietly.

I checked the other two ax-ramblers and found nothing new, and once again there seemed no way to fire up their engines.

Defeated for the moment, I padded to the edge of the roof that was guarded by a high barricade. On tiptoe I could lean on it to see over it to the streets below. Like the stairwell, the streetlights were few and weak. I stayed for a while, thinking.

In the distance, at the end of the straight boulevard of ruined buildings and rubble, lay a small lake. Leading down that road and into the gleam of water, was a wide, wet trail. Orcs or other people milled about at the edge of that lake. It seemed a dangerous place to be, if a creature had come from there.

The screams had ceased. I was struck by the surrealness of a crowd of orc warriors waving axes in the middle of this city of ancient skyscrapers. Had these once thrived with clerks and secretaries, and people bearing the equivalent of cups of coffee as they hurried to work?

Maybe, just maybe, I could find my way out of here on foot, if I was careful as a mouse in a barn full of cats.

"Questions, questions," I murmured to myself. "Where is that tentacle monster, and do orcs have night vision? And where can I find some clothes?" Having decided to go look for a room with cupboards full of clothes, I turned. There must be something.

Behind me stood Kragga, waiting with a no-nonsense stare of doom. Looming, basically. "Greetings, Char."

I gasped. "Where did you learn to sneak?" I debated whether to run, again, and switched my focus to beyond him. No one else was here.

"Let's not do that." He snagged my wrist with a grip hard as iron.

I tugged, could not get free, and caught sight of his determined expression. It made a tense thrill trickle up through my belly... as if I liked this.

Which I always had, on Earth. Being caught by a man, held down, or tied up in pursuit of a kinky scene. For the first time since our abduction to this starship, I felt my old fetishes and needs resurrect themselves.

Being trapped and made to take whatever my dominant wished upon me, almost always hit my sweet spot of kink.

An orc, though? Had my standards fallen, or had they simply gone sideways and light-years.

"Come. I have something for you."

"A present?" I said brightly. Gods knew where my courage came from. Had my subconscious decided Kragga was safe?

"No. Punishment."

"Goodie," I whispered, almost meaning it because, I simply did.

He shot me an odd look.

8

KRAGGA

"Where were you going?"

"To see Isolde," she answered, mouth awry in petulance.

"Of course you were going to see the other girl who is human, who lives hours, days, of travel away. And you must go past the sea of tentacles that kill, and the riots, and the murderous mob of alphas, who might tear apart a small omega before they fuck her to death anyway." I paused and spun her back into the metal barricade. "An omega like you. I would call you stupid, but I guess it's just ignorance."

"How was I to know you had tentacle monsters?"

I opened my mouth, closed it, sighed. "Truly, I didn't know that one, either. It's some sort of aberration. An unknown, though the deep tunnels of the ship have always harbored strange creatures. No one has catalogued them all. But that was not from a tunnel."

I faced her outward and pointed. "You see the wet trail?"

"I did."

"After it swatted Mog, who has recovered, it returned to that inlet of the sea."

"He what-the-hell recovered? That is a sea?" She seemed amazed and genuinely interested.

"He did, and it is."

We had run outside the banquet hall, only to find the creature had retreated across the façade of the buildings, reversed its journey, and crawled along the fronts before it dropped into the street several blocks down. Some red orcs were already chasing it, so we left them to the work. Though large, it had not killed anyone. A hunting party might be best sent out in daylight, in any case.

"Yes." I towed her toward the nearest ax-rambler. "I will show you the core and the land and sea between us and Isolde. But first, you will say why you ran from me."

"Because you're an orc, and I am a human? Is that not enough? You let your brothers handle me."

Without clothes and dressed in only chains and a collar, she was far too tempting, but I stopped and steadied her, with my hands cupping her shoulders. I studied her, cautiously, without looking lower than her neck. For that I deserved an award. "That bothered you?"

"Of course it did."

"You climaxed!"

"Beside the point. On Earth we do not share our bed partners unless there is mutual agreement."

"Hmmm. I see." I thought perhaps I did. Letting Vagrax and the other two do what they did had been agonizing, until she came. After that I had been too distracted to care, much.

I stared past her.

"I will not allow that again. I promise."

"An orc promise?" She sucked in a long breath, and I half expected her to ask if that meant anything.

"My word is true. Even though we orcs are mostly seen as the grunts of the warrior class, we get the job done, and we are generally honest. We follow through on promises." I moved in on her, finally, uptilted her chin. "Okay?"

"I'll have to recalibrate. In our stories, orcs were the evil minions who followed a dark lord."

"Minions? Though we do like to follow. It is the orc way." I was sure I did not like this minion word. I guided her until we reached the side of the ax-rambler. "Take care to avoid the sharp things. Up." I smacked her very naked ass and only shrugged at her glare before I lifted her high so she could scramble onto the roof. "Worse is coming!"

I thought I heard a quiet scoff.

Why did I get the feeling we were reaching an understanding of each other? I stared at her ass then joined her on the roof, clambering up while dodging the metal fins projecting from the vehicle's upper section.

The roof of the rambler was black, same as the rest, and there was room for us and the gun platform. The scope was still on top of the long cannon, as was the crossbow attachment. The scope could stay. I lifted off the crossbow and laid it well aside, so we could not trip over it. Thankfully, the two dragon missiles had been removed.

Char seemed bemused by all the pieces.

"This is normal," I informed her.

"It is? Like Boy Scouts, I guess. Be prepared."

"Indeed." After, I raised the flex arm of the gun mount to its full height, I sat on the broad leather seat. "Here. Now." When she turned to see what I meant, I pulled her down and over my lap.

"I am going to show you the sights, but first you need this."

I raised one hand, with my other hand weighing her down at the waist and pinning her to my thighs. She squirmed, of course, flailed with her arms, and tried to rise.

It was difficult to hold back my grin, but I did.

"Hey! Wait. Is this fair?"

"Did you run when told to go to my room?"

She wriggled a little but twisted to peer at me. I was big enough that only the ends of her fingers might touch the roof while she lay on my legs. I raised one knee to force her to hold my lower leg instead.

"I suppose, but you are my enemy. Is that not a reason? You cut off your enemy's heads with axes."

"The ones who deserve it, yes," I said quietly. "We are not enemies, Char. I will never be that to you. I promise."

"Oh. Awkward. As in very," she muttered. "You see, maybe we are, but you don't know it."

What was this?

"I've done things you cannot imagine, Kragga. Bad things."

"Those I will forgive, but not running." I pointed that out to regain control of the conversation.

"If you knew—"

"Tell me it then, afterward."

I raised my hand and delivered the first smack to her ass, then did the other cheek. Again, she struggled to get free. Ten more of my restrained blows brought her to gasping and another five to giving up and occasionally whining.

It was an entirely satisfying whine, according to my rigid cock.

"Perhaps you thought I would be lenient, Char. I will not be. Not when it gives me a reason to redden you here." Lovingly, I ran my hand over the luscious globe. The pinkness did not show well, at night. "Blue lighting does not suit your ass," I muttered. And it was such a cute, rounded one, too.

"Can I get up now?"

"So polite, suddenly?"

She said nothing, so I slipped my hand between her legs and found her cunt a sloppy mess of omega fluids. Interesting, even enlightening?

"Is it just being near me? Or the spanking?" Would she answer truthfully?

She cleared her throat, and I felt her entrance clamp in and release as I teased her below, not entering her, simply circling and playing there.

"I love the feel of your swollen folds. You want me, but we are not ready yet."

"We? Fuck." She coughed as if choking. I'd slipped into her to the first knuckle. "Oh. I… don't mind that. At all."

Her squirming became more urgent, and she impaled herself deeper.

"It's you, being near you. Okay?"

"Use my name, please, Char."

"It is you, and it is this fucking omega thing, and your touch, your smell. Even if it's odd."

I let her ramble on, for I was enjoying being able to penetrate her, casually, while she talked.

"Your erection under me, too."

I chuckled.

"And yes," she added in a soft voice. "The spanking. I always liked those unless they were brutal ones."

I leaned over her and kissed behind her ear. "I can do brutal. Be careful in future. If you run, it had better be prearranged, or else."

"Okay." Her answer was soft, and she shuddered under me, stirring my already rock-hard cock.

"Stand up for me."

She eased herself off my lap and stood before me, looking a little ashamed.

"Are you worried I will do something bad?"

"Maybe." Her frown was tiny and disappeared almost instantly. "It's just odd." She looked up and found my eyes.

"That you are human, and I am orc?" I settled my hands around her waist as she nodded. "Don't be afraid, though ashamed has its appeal. I wonder what I can do to get that response again?"

At her wide eyes, I had to smile.

"Then it is a yes."

"Hmph."

"Spread your legs for me, and I'll remove these little chains. Their purpose is over, and I want to see you with nothing on you, because I'm going to fuck you for the first time." I reached down to edge my finger into that wet little hole again. "As much as I can."

That talk was enough to leave her wide of eye and complacent. I stripped her, casually, until all I could see was her.

"Good girl," I murmured.

It was agony to make myself wait, but all I did was undo my pants and free my erection. It distracted her as I placed my hands on her and slowly ran them down her shoulders, beneath her breasts, cupping them and circling both her nipples before I ran my hands over her hips.

Only then did I pause to inhale and lift her by the waist.

"Beg me to impale you."

Her gulp was obvious. "Please?" Her legs were wriggling.

"You want me to stick my large, spiked cock inside you?" I was taunting her, and it was more fun than I'd had for ages.

"Yes! Please?" Her eyebrows rose high, and she drew her legs up and opened them, exposing herself fully.

"Hmmm. This first." And I brought her pussy to my mouth and settled her legs over my shoulders. I growled then applied my tongue to her clit, leisurely swiping it from cunt hole, over clit then around it before I gave that nub of pleasure one drawn-out suck. Then I ceased and looked up.

The mewl she gave me, a needy, desperate sound, and the shock on her face were highly satisfying.

"More? Let me see where to begin. Be patient. You are the first human I've eaten."

"Oh gods. Please? Yes, more. Do it. Hmm?" She inhaled and held her breath, studying me, waiting, only squirming a little. I could feel her slipperiness on my shoulders and chest.

I wished I had brought one of the big dildos, but my fingers would do.

I leaned in and licked her again, slowly toggling her clit with my tongue, circling it, teasing her, then applying myself fully to engulfing it and stimulating her to climax.

She moaned loudly and tossed back her head as she arched. She tried a few times to wrench my face even closer.

But I merely tongued and sucked her at my own pace, edging down to nothing while I probed her pussy and wormed four fingers into her, one at a time. And when I knew they would fit, I stuffed in all of them at once.

Char stiffened and groaned as I pushed them full depth. My hand would not fit, but four fingers was close to the girth of my newly enlarged, alpha-sized cock.

"Fuck, fuck, more. Oh." Again, she threw back her head, tightened her thigh grip on me, and gave a throaty groan as her body began to buck.

She was in the throes of orgasming, so I jammed my four fingers harder into her, pumping in and out a little while she rocked on my shoulders and gave a few last cries,

I held her higher, slid her legs off my shoulders, and lowered Char to my lap, until my cock found her entry, and could let her body weight sink her inexorably onto my dick.

"That." I grunted and hip thrust, made her squeal. "Feels…" I thrust and gripped on her waist. She found my head and pulled me down to her mouth.

Kissing her still, I managed to squeeze a third inside of myself, spikes and all.

"Fuck." Feeling strangled by the sensations, I swallowed more curses before blurting, "Fuck, that's good."

She was tight, as expected, tight enough to crush onto what I could fit in there.

Did I care? No.

Her inner spasms were heaven by themselves. We kissed, messily, wetly, mouths sliding and breathing heat.

With every kiss, every sigh, every wanton look she gave me, every time I caressed her breasts, I shoved myself in a little further.

"Stop!" she finally squeaked and met my eyes. "That's too much. It hurts!" Her small hands were wrapped firmly over my shoulder and partly around my neck, and her nails were digging in.

I gritted my teeth. "Okay. Enough."

My last few thrusts went no deeper but brought me to the brink of exploding.

I held it in, held it in… and then I came, grunting, and she gasped again and whimpered, and her cunt squeezed onto me, triggering a new wave of come. The pressure inside her eased, and a flood of my *basja* rushed from her and onto my legs. I reached beneath and scooped some of it onto my palm before carrying it to her mouth.

This time, she lapped from me without a command. She tilted her head and raised herself to kiss my tusk, with her mouth slowly sucking on it before she said something so quietly that I missed it. It was one of the sexiest things I had ever seen.

My cock was lesser by then but still inside her.

She eyed me hesitantly then whispered. "Did I do something wrong, kissing you there.

"No. That was…" I shook my head and smiled. "That was perfect. Each time we do this it will be easier for you, and I will go deeper. Do you understand?"

"Mmm." Char sank down and stretched her arms to hug my chest, then curled her head around so she could nibble on one of the rings that pierced my left nipple.

"We will stay here a while. When you're ready, I will show you the moon through the scope, and everything up there that seems worth looking at. I want you to know our ship because this is your home now. This is your world."

She inhaled and shifted on me but remained silent.

9

CHAR

The mess under us on the ax-rambler's roof and on his pants must be substantial, but Kragga didn't seem to care so I did my best to ignore it. If we slipped, we might slice ourselves on the spikes, but I was beginning to think orcs were careless of some sorts of risks, or they failed to think ahead.

Maybe I could compensate by thinking ahead for both of us?

Maybe I should reconsider happily linking myself to an orc. He did have a leaning toward being a romantic, though. It was sweet, in a big, green, orcish way.

When told to, I rested my eyes into the scope, wedging my face in place until everything above shimmied into focus.

"There. Can you see the moon?" he asked.

"Yes. It's too huge to miss."

"If we waited until morning, I could show you how the sun lights up, and the yellow eats the blue. It's an amazing sight, and I've seen it a thousand times."

It felt as if I were at a tourist hotspot, and Kragga was my guide. It was novel and weird and exciting. For once I didn't wish to be back on Earth.

I didn't fear him anymore—a sobering thought because I should be scared.

"What's behind the moon?" I knew there were, theoretically, more houses there, and the species called mauleons, and Isolde—providing she was still alive. "Mauleons?"

"Yes." Kragga reached in front of my eyes and adjusted the scope. The focus slowly fuzzed out on the moon and made the more distant part of the core turn into a little map of streets. *Night-time there, too.*

There were black scars where houses must have once existed. Most of the fires seemed to have been extinguished, but I wondered what had happened to Isolde. Could she have died? A clot of what must be people swarmed across one section, filling the streets, and I swung the scope to the side, and found sea. As if by not seeing the anarchy I would make everything fine?

"I see the sea," I said quietly, trying to conceal my pain. My worry was that I had caused this.

Should I feel guilty if aliens had died? Or if my friend had? Yes. Unless I was a fool and heartless. Isolde had been abducted from Earth and brought here because she had followed me. My eyes were tearing up, and I pulled away from the scope to wipe under them with the knuckle of one finger. And I found Kragga watching me.

"Are you okay?"

"The scope made my eyes water."

He looked dubious.

"The sea?" I asked.

"Yes?"

"What lives there? Not just your tentacle monster, I'd bet."

"No. Not just it. The gogogians live there. They love to be around other species, humans and mauleons mostly, run the markets. They trade. Rumor says they found this starship and sold it to us centuries ago.

"Huh." I knew so little of this place, this starship.

Abducted, brought here, caged along with Isolde and other women, then on-sold to Vedrock and taken to his ship, and none of that had educated me much about this giant ship, that was the mothership to many others and home to tens of thousands of humanoids.

Wait. Were the gogogians humanoids? They lived in the sea, after all.

"What do gogogians look like?"

"They are larger than humans but smaller than us, have tentacles, can sustain themselves in outer space for some time without protection—"

"Tentacles?"

"Yes. And no, they are nothing like the monster today."

"But… maybe a relative?"

Kragga sighed and pulled the scope around, so I had to abandon looking through it.

"No. That thing was crawling across the face of towers. It was two stories high."

I almost said, *a big relative then*, but refrained. The idea niggled though, since the connection seemed possible, to me, if not to an orc.

"Let me show you more things across the other side. You understand we're on the inside of a cylinder not a globe, and that over there was the markets? Or is. The gogogians run some shops there…"

I zoned out a little.

It was obvious Kragga was trying to distract me from what he thought was a silly theory. He was managing to distract me in other ways. The funny, annoying, and wondrous thing was that since I was still on his lap and naked, every touch of his hands on my body…

Every fleeting glance of his breath over my hair…

Every movement of him behind me and beneath me felt not just *good* but comforting. Was I hoping too much here? Leaping to dumb conclusions? This was an orc, yet I felt safe in his lap and in his arms, with his heart thudding and reassuring me whenever I rested my ear on his chest.

Love was not safety. Safety did not equal love.

Then I realized what he was saying.

There was nothing much left to eat in Rishnak, because the supply lines were down and the mechlings said that it was the same across the sea.

If he was a person, these were his people, too.

"They say the whole galaxy is suffering problems like here, but someone will fix this. We wait and there will arise a solution."

"Someone?"

I opened my mouth to speak against this fatalistic solution to a vast, complex problem.

A problem I had caused, yes?

The horror finally dawned on me. I had killed many people, caused starvation across an entire galaxy, and murder, and worse, if there was worse. I may have killed millions.

"The rumor also is that Vedrock had something to do with this—"

"I did this." *In revenge.* I closed my mouth and pinched it in. *Me.* Not just revenge, maybe, but the results made my reasons useless.

"Why would you think that, Char?"

I shook my head.

"You will tell me why you said that. Now."

I turned in his lap. The stern determination on his face almost made me spill everything I had done, then and there. "I will, but please, please give me time."

Heavens and hells, I needed time.

"You expect me to trust you, my newly acquired Earth female?"

When he put it like that…

How could I ask him, a strange orc to do this?

Hesitantly, I took one of his hands, and it was twice as large as mine and possibly thrice as heavy, and I clasped it between mine. I dared to meet his eyes again. "Please trust me for a while, Kragga. I swear… this newly acquired Earth female now called Char, I vow to tell you. Trust me?"

"Well." He studied where I held him, then grumbled out, "I will then. For a while. But not forever."

"Okay." I nodded. Then I lay down against him again and put my ear to his chest to listen to his heart.

10

CHAR

I'd thought the threat was not genuine when Kragga ordered the other orcs to bring a cage to his study. Yet here I was, inside it.

The bars were rusty and left orange marks on my hands whenever I held them, and the cage's roof height gave me barely enough room to sit upright, especially with the cushions under my rear. Since this room was wall to wall in old books, I wanted out.

"I could learn to read them," I sang out to Kragga, where he sat at a desk inspecting papers, with a pair of little black spectacles balanced on his nose. It looked both ridiculous and sexy for an orc to wear those. It made him seem respectable and thoughtful, and for some ungodly reason, I found it hot as fuck.

The books on his desk were piled up and less dilapidated than those on the shelves.

"I doubt that. Those." He raised his chin to indicate the shelves of books. "Are partly from whoever was living here a hundred years ago. The only new ones are these." He tapped the books near him.

I clasped my hands over my knees, and drew them closer to my body, fully aware it would be giving him an eyeful of what lay between my legs. Being kept naked made clothes choices easier, I had to admit, and ditto flirting with orcs. I was probably insane to want to.

"So, you all run and built a starship but still use paper books and wear spectacles?"

"Sometimes. The comms are bad and down at this moment anyway. Luckily, the mechlings have their own network. As to these?" He briefly lifted the specs from his nose. "My eyes are not good at short distances. Surgery and synth eyes," he added offhandedly, "… can lead to problems." He shot me a teasing smile. "Miss Human with the open slutty legs. I see that fine."

I refused to blush. Besides, that surgery comment was more alarming. "What? What problems?"

"You're fine. Besides, there was little to no alternative."

True. I might have died. I could recall the throwing up I'd suffered on the *Social Deviance* in awful detail, and even now it brought a sour taste to my mouth. I grimaced.

That communication remark though—did that mean they had some sort of network with data mostly in the cloud? It must do.

"What are you studying?"

"Law."

"Fuck me," I said half to myself.

"Willingly." He looked up again. A wave of desire washed in and made me aware of who had the power here. "Hmmm."

I froze. Did I really want more of that huge dick of his inside me so soon? No. Fuck no. I was still sore. "I meant I was studying to go to do law on Earth."

"You studied law so as to then study it?"

"Pre-law. Sort of, yes, but not."

"Confusing." He went back to his papers.

I squirmed around and put hands to the rusty bars. "Could I not come and sit up there with you? I mean, platonically. No touching." I frowned. "I'm still sore."

"I'm not surprised. If you want to sit here, you know what to do. Your promise. Are you ready to tell me why you said, *I did it*?" He peered sternly over the specs, observing me from my toes to the top of my head, like a schoolteacher chastising a student, while also considering bending that student over the desk.

"Soon? I guess?" I hoped that hadn't sounded like a whine.

How could I tell him? It gave me ulcers thinking about telling Kragga of the day I fucked the universe. I didn't want to be stuck on a spike, or shot into the cold vacuum of space, minus a suit. Or whatever orcs in space did to their enemies. I also hated the idea of becoming the enemy of this orc, in particular."

"Thought so." He wrote something using a rust-colored pen.

"I could help you?"

He grunted.

I heard a tap, outside the room. It sounded as if it were the balcony door, directly opposite the open door to this room. I crawled over and pressed my head to the far corner of the cage, then heard Kragga rise. His chair glided backward.

He padded over to stand beside the cage, then kneeled and inserted his arm between the bars to place a hand over my mouth.

"*Shhh.* Stay there." He shot me a grin then walked away, with an axe held nonchalantly low and swinging from his left hand.

Stay there? *Haha, funny.*

I frowned. Did orcs pull axes from their asses? They always seemed to procure an axe from somewhere unknown. It must have been next to the desk. He exited through the double-wide door entry, slipped to the right, and disappeared from view. I could see through the opening and past the living room, to balcony doors and the sky full of buildings. Did Kragga think the tentacle monster had returned? Surely those creatures smashed through doors and didn't merely tap?

I wasn't up to date with monster etiquette. How flippant that sounded. Living here was rubbing off on me.

On Earth, the merest noise in the night had made me drag my sheet over my head and clutch my phone, ready to call the cops or scream. I ran a finger around the inside of my collar, brushing by the blunt spikes. On Earth, being molested by strangers had been a crime. Here, it was apparently a fancy part of a ceremony.

I heard raised voices and then Kragga re-entered and waited by the door, followed by… something weird. And on an alien starship weird really meant WTF.

I had seen mechlings before, but this was much bigger, and it talked.

It was a robot of sorts, but spidery, with multiple legs reaching to the floor from a green box, then on top of that was a blue bug-shaped shell with more smaller legs, followed by a white globe possibly intended as the head. The entire robot was a little shorter than me.

I had decided the globe was its head because it was on top, and because someone had drawn a face on it with a mouth, eyes with lashes, and some surreal red swirls at the back that might be a sketch of hair.

"Hello! Charlotte! It is I, Quinn, your mechling doc." Its next words came out low and shaky, as if it shared a terrible secret. "How are your eyes?"

Kragga caught up with him and rapped a knuckle on his... its head. "Don't scare her, Quinn! This is the mechling who did your eyes, Char. He did a very good job on them, too. You have no problems?"

He cocked an eyebrow. I shook my head then transferred attention to this creature that seemed a mutant version of my worst robot nightmares.

This had cut out my eyes?

"You have a new bottom part, Quinn?" Kragga asked.

Legs clicking, the mechling trotted up to me and the cage and folded itself to be on my level.

"I do! This bottom bit is a different mechling, the green part of me. I thought it best to be of a good height. Do not concern yourself, he is not an awoken."

"Awoken?" I stared past Quinn at Kragga as he, too, lowered himself, so that he could squat outside the cage.

"It means he is a sentient creature, like us. It's a new sort of mechling." Kragga frowned. "A virus was sent out by another creature called Smorg, and it freed some mechlings to become self-aware. If you ever meet him, I will introduce you."

"Smorg, our glorious savior, yes, yes." Quinn unfolded a pincer limb with a slim black cylinder at the end. "Look into the light, Char. I will check for defects."

I stared at the glowing end of the cylinder. Why not?

"Oh, yes. Good. Yes, just so. Good." The mechling angled the device here and there, seemingly examining my eyes. "You have nothing to complain of?"

"No. They make noises sometimes, but that is all."

"Excellent results. They seem to function perfectly." It stepped backward to peer up at Kragga. "I admit, I am here to ask you a favor, also."

After a last glance my way, Kragga went to his desk, rolled the chair clear of it and to the side, then sat. "Ask. I will try to help you, the same as you helped Char. Though..." He leaned forward. "I see you've drawn features on yourself now? Why the change of heart?"

The mechling swayed from side to side. "I hope to gain empathy with orcs, mauleons, humans. I believe you prefer faces?"

"We do. Someone could advise you on that, though. The art style is a bit rough, and if not done well, it may scare people rather than attract them."

"I realize this. You are being polite." Quinn sighed. "As to my favor, it regards personhood for awoken mechlings. We wish to submit a request to the courts through Grut, asking for all awoken mechlings to be granted personhood, en masse."

"In one go? And in the middle of this... mess?" Kragga clasped his hands behind his head. "A difficult task. Similar to the process when a new species asks, when one is found on a new planet or system?"

"Yes. Is it possible?"

"You need precedents." They both swung my way. "If your laws are like ours on Earth." Then cautiously, I said, "I could help you do it?"

Quinn looked at both of us.

Kragga spoke up first. "I can help you, Quinn. Yes, it's possible to use those other requests as templates. We need to prove sentience. This submission would likely be only a first step, then you would have to submit to testing to prove what we assert is true."

Wow, this orc knew legalese.

"Good, good. Whatever you need from me and us, Kragga."

"I will do the research, and your mechling network will be essential. The *Filthy Lucre*'s network keeps crashing."

"I'll send a mechling to be your aide, tomorrow. May I ask, what brought her out of her semi-conscious state? She seemed permanently impaired."

"My come did. She begged me for it. I gave it."

I covered my mouth, as if that was a way to hide. The shame of what I had done brought heat to my cheeks, and yet this was a robot and he was an orc. It was stupid to feel shame.

"I see! Interesting. There are reports regarding the effects of various drugs on the alphas in other areas of the galaxy. That the chemicals in alpha orc semen could do this to an omega makes me wonder. Can we reverse this and use a drug on alphas to calm them?"

Kragga looked mystified.

Me? It seemed a farfetched theory. Was Quinn planning to feed come to alphas? I would love to be an onlooker to *that*.

"Also, thank you for your help, Kragga. Thank you so much, dear orc."

Dear orc. Those words sounded like they should never be paired together. I smiled and almost giggled. It was as if the orc was a friend of this awoken mechling, and if that was so, if these two trusted one another, what else was possible? Especially, what else was possible between a human girl and a big bad orc?

Once Doc Quinn had left—and he climbed the outside of the building again rather than stairs or elevator—Kragga came to the cage and went on one knee. He leaned his arm on the top. "You can help if you want to, Char, but there are conditions."

"Don't run? Of course it's a yes."

He smirked, which always made his tusks look bigger and meaner. "No. I need to spread your pussy wider so I can fit next time."

Eeep. And also fuck. "Oh. I see." I swallowed. Damn him. "That's it?"

"It is a steel spreader and is normally one used to make females of a smaller species accommodate an orc's phallus."

"Okay. I understood the first time." *Okay* was an under-bloody-statement.

"You would sit next to me, on a chair, with what I choose to use today, inside you." He unfolded to his full height. "Choose. Cage or this. Of course, I will do it eventually, anyway. This way I might be gentler."

What?

What did I say to that?

"I, *umm*, gentler?"

He strolled to the desk, sat on the edge, and folded his arms. "Perhaps."

No smile this time, simply a dark intent in those yellow eyes.

He was making me choose when, not if. And fuck me, if this wasn't exceptionally teasing. I rather knew I wanted this, but also that it sounded dubious, unsafe, as well as hot. This was volunteering to be defiled, and that wasn't my kink, was it? Yes, yes it was.

"Well?"

"Okay," I squeaked, and found I'd wrapped my hands around the bars. I dropped them to my lap and frowned at the rust on my palms.

"Good. Don't go anywhere, will you. I'll be back with the spreader."

The. Spreader. I blinked.

As if I could go elsewhere. Asshole orc. What had I gotten myself into? When he returned, a rectangular case hung from one hand. With his other hand, he carried a metal chair with armrests.

"Look what I found in my *jus-rak* chest." He raised the case then positioned the new chair next to his, behind the desk. "Close your eyes, girl. This is to be a surprise. Though I will say its big and metal and looks as if I could use it as a weapon."

That was a mindfuck, I told myself. I mouthed *asshole*, and closed my eyes to slits, wondering if I could get away with pretending.

"Close them or I put a hood over your head."

I shut them properly.

He opened the cage, drew me out, and guided me to the desk, where he stopped me at the chair, and put my hand on the armrest.

"Open your eyes." I thought he didn't want me to see this terrible device?

A dark green double dildo sat on the chair, sticking up in a threatening manner, mostly because it was *large*. It appeared to be rubbery and was not metal, and not the evil device Kragga had described.

I shot him a glare. "You lied."

"It was fun." He grinned momentarily. "Now sit on it. Or else."

He had left the *or else* open-ended. I gestured. "There are two parts to it, though. Two?"

I knew what the intent was but hoping for the best was an integral part of my soul.

"All the better to fuck both your holes, Char."

My hopeful look of cute innocence was met with an unyielding expression and tilted eyebrow.

Damn.

"Sit on it, or else. There really is a metal version in my chest."

"Lube?"

He leaned in and said to my ear, "You and I know you don't need any."

Those words, that mouth near me then kissing my neck, and the brief scrape of his tusks, I sighed and melted. My clit popped up like the obedient slut it was.

I drew a deep breath and maneuvered myself between desk and chair, then I wedged my teeth on my bottom lip and carefully lowered myself onto those two dicks. I wouldn't fit—it was a given, but the thing tapered, and the longer I sat, the further it would insert itself.

Kragga went around to the back of the chair, and just as the tips of the dildos found my entrances, he grasped my breasts. "Slowly, girl. I have you."

"Fuck you," I ventured, whimpering as the evil dildos penetrated further. If I let all my weight go…

Kragga laughed. "I heard that." And he leaned his forearms onto me, urging me downward. I squeaked, and my eyes opened wide before I jammed them shut.

"Fuck, fuck, fuck."

"Yes, that is the idea."

He released me, and I sank as far as those fake dicks would allow. My hands had wrapped over the armrests, and I cried out as I tried to accustom myself to this invasion. Moving made them worm about, too. "Oh fuck. Can I please get up?"

"No."

Swiftly, he strapped one arm to the armrest then did the other side, though I tried to escape. Resistance was, apparently, futile. I stared at the straps.

"Let us study now. Quietly."

"Oh, you are an asshole."

"I know. I also know I'm going to be inside yours soon, so your insults will go unrewarded. No spanking, or not until I'm satisfied you've sat on those for long enough."

Then he had the gall to seat himself again and study his papers.

I settled, somewhat. My panting and whines lessened, but it was difficult to remain utterly quiet.

"Nipple clamps," Kragga said.

Distraught, I swiveled my head. "What did you say?"

"Keep distracting me with noise and nipple clamps will happen."

Now I was torn. How did he manage to appall and attract me in one short sentence? I loved random sadism, if done within the right relationship. Clearly, my concept of a good relationship had mutated and run away to hide under the floorboards.

I swallowed and attempted to ignore the flurries of lust that simmered deep. Every time I breathed, those rubbery cocks shifted and found new slutty nerve endings. I moaned, very softly, then went silent, absorbing my desire, tucking it away in the back end of my mind. My pussy clenched on the enormous dildo.

My ass was less enthusiastic, but the sensations were… melding together.

Concentrate.

"Okay." I sat forward, clenched, hissed, but looked to him. "What can I do to help?"

"I didn't really expect anything, and you are tied up."

Asshole, again.

"I can read."

"Hmmm." He smirked and took a book from a pile and opened it before me. "How will you turn pages? Though you could look for acts relevant to this." He slid a paper nearer and adjacent to the book.

"I'll signal—tap the armrest with my fingernail, and you turn the page."

"Innovative little human. And determined. Very well."

And so, it began. An hour went by. An hour that fluctuated between actual, real work on this mechling submission and well, me squirming on two dicks. That Kragga now and then slid his hand through the opening beneath the armrest frame and over my thigh then between my legs. Did not help. Shockingly.

I found myself gaping at his hand, again, at where his fingers held my clit in thrall. I was neglecting the page.

"How far in are they?" he said, still reading the book before him.

"In? Oh. Well." My gasp was automatic. Kragga's fingers had slid to where the first dildo impaled me. "I don't know." I squirmed again and regretted it. I would surely split open if it went any deeper.

"We should find out."

He left his book open, slid off his chair to his knees, and turned my chair in order to study me with that deviant smile of his.

"You will need rehydrating." He gripped beneath my thighs and slowly hauled the chair closer, with me on it. He tilted the chair then hummed before saying, "Needs more… depth."

"Wait, Don't—"

"*Shhh.* I'm not forcing them deeper. Or not yet." And he bent over and stuck his ugly tusked green face over my pussy, and barely touched my clit with his tongue tip.

Lust slammed me like a force-ten hurricane. I moaned loudly, arching even though I could go nowhere, and it made the dildos cram into all the wrong and right places. The back of my head pressed into the chair.

"That easy?" I heard him say, distantly, past the thrum of my blood and the creak of the chair as I stiffened and put stresses on it no furniture maker could have predicted. I needed that long fucking orc tongue, that hot mouth, the hardness of those tusks. "More?"

I may have said *ungh* at best, and my legs were trying to wrap about him but his arms were in the way and his chest too broad, so they slipped off. Then he applied his entire mouth to sucking me off.

The room blanked as I was thrown into the pulsating mindblast of an orgasm. It left me spluttering for air, disorientated, and limp. He unstrapped my arms and pulled me off the chair, then positioned me facedown over the desk. Foggy of brain, I was vaguely sorry for the books I might be wetting with drool and my fluids, for the pages I might be tearing as he crammed his dick into me, pushing me froward as he thrust. I was shunted across the desk and back. Filled to bursting, I wept and grunted and clutched at things. When he came, the mess leaked and pooled warmly beneath me. Exhausted and hoarse from crying out, I felt for the table edges then for him. Finding his muscular body still behind me, feeling him lean on me again, I ceased trying to move.

I could stay there forever, satisfied, and sore. When he withdrew, my pussy spasmed in, and there was nothing. I was unfilled for the first time in hours, and it seemed wrong. I was unbearably empty.

Then he lay on the desk on his back beside me, muttering curses and holding his dick. Frowning, I waited for him to explain. Some papers had been crumpled when he landed on the desk, but mostly he'd sent books tumbling to the floor. He cursed his dick some more and groaned.

At last, he fell silent except for a last, "Ouch."

He rolled over and stared at my face for a while before gently untangling my hair from my mouth and nose.

"Hello."

"Why were you in pain?"

"Me? I had a knot on my dick. It happens with alpha and omega sex, sometimes, but I think it's supposed to happen inside you. And so, my dick was not happy."

"Ohhh."

"You're still not taking all of me, pretty thing. We will figure it out."

We? I smiled. "Sure. I don't know how, but please not the metal dildo."

He chuckled. "Never. Not unless you're a really bad-bad girl for Kragga." Then he pushed two fingers into my mouth, and I licked at them, reveling in the taste of our lovemaking, in his blunt wide fingernails. My tongue could even feel the whorls of his fingerprints. "All of it, Char. Lick it all off."

I stared back at this giant, green orc with the dark sense of humor, struck by awe and an emotion I refused to acknowledge... yet. I knew I liked him, though. I liked him more than was sensible, more than all the good men I had found on Earth, and there had been some I'd almost loved.

And here I was unable to tell him the truth about my words.

11

CHAR

It was early morning at the dock markets, and the pseudo sun was shining a hearty yellow down on us, from the middle of the core. I was getting used to the terminology. We were on the inside of a cylinder, and at one end was the command center of the *Filthy Lucre*. At the other, I guessed, must be the engines. I should ask if there was a map, a diagram of the starship.

If it were truly made from a hollowed-out fossil of a giant space-faring dragon... that actually helped. Seas and tunnels and upside-down cities on a starship? I shook my head to dispel my daydream.

This market was populated by orcs, a few mechlings, and some humans. The busy paths and the bright colors of the stalls contrasted with the quietness of a barely rippling sea. Beneath much of the market was a timber dock, and running out from that was a jetty that stretched far into the water.

Although no one was swimming or boating, I had to wonder at their logic.

"Do visits from tentacled sea monsters not make people rethink the safety of this?" I asked Kragga.

Though on his insistence I wore my collar, he only held my hand, now and then, and kept me by his side. He did scowled or grumbled loudly when other males stopped to give me too close a study. It was novel to be with such a protective, jealous male. Right now, he was examining the wares of a food seller. Fruit? Vegetable? A rare fungus? I squinted. The basketball-sized globes were bright pink, smelled disgusting, and had stubby orange spikes around them, like a baby sea mine. I decided it looked fruit-ish. Of course, orcs would eat that.

When he didn't answer my question, I turned to watch a small, passing crowd.

A few young orcs ran about between the adults, ducking, weaving, and screaming in joy like any human children might. Tag must be a universal game. It looked normal, if I discounted the green skin, tusks, and multiple sharp weapons. And yet, when I really looked, bandaged wounds and fresh scars showed on some of the males. Their faces bore a stoic grimness, though these were orcs, so that might be okay. And the stalls? Was it normal for their shelves to be so low in produce?

I scanned the surrounding skyline of ruined buildings. No fires or smoke showed, there was that. Was I reading too much into this? An ominous undertone seeped into this bright, merry scene, and I half expected to hear the beat of jungle drums or for spiders to creep atop the towers, or maybe for gigantic tentacles to tear one apart.

Something wicked this way comes. Yes, that. My heart stalled for a second, but nothing happened.

Nothing but for this mildly busy market beside the tentacle monster's sea.

I'd been hoping to see gogogians, but there had been none I could identify. How similar were they to that monster? Surely their tentacles would make them stand out?

"Come." Kragga took my hand again. "I have a dagger stall to visit then we can have lunch at the water's edge."

"And dangle our legs over the stone like bait for monsters?"

He grinned. "Ahh that."

"Isn't it a bit fatalistic to hold this here?"

He shrugged. "It is the orc—"

"Way," I filled in. "I see." I also eyerolled.

"We like to live life as it comes. That creature never hurt anyone. Mog recovered. All it did was drop a few signs on people."

We reached the dagger merchant, and the stall was about far more than daggers. Bins filled with books, axes, daggers, curtain material... what-the-fuck... and other things kept me roving along the aisles. Kragga was still stuck procrastinating at the display of shiny sharp things, of course.

I ran into a being totally rife with wriggly pink tentacles with purple suckers. Some of those tentacles were thick as a coffee cup. It was a vaguely cone shape, from top to bottom, and came up to my ears, at best. It also squelched when it walked or glided over the floor.

I gulped and stared. "Are you a gogogian?"

"Indeed I am. My name is Datteo. May I help you, miss human?"

"I'm Charlotte, or Char, for short." It was odd using the nickname Kragga had given me but even odder talking to this gogogian who had a piggy face in the middle of smaller tentacles. "I don't think I need help?" The last word came out squeaky and with a disarming grin.

"Pray, do not worry about me. We are not generally aggressive, unless selling you an item. Hehehe. Agreed, Kragga?"

They knew each other?

"Yes, to harmless," he sang out. "No to selling her anything."

Datteo squirmed in a half-circle around me, and I turned to follow.

"I like the clothes. Very, uhhh." It held a tentacle under its mouth. "Sexy but kickass?"

"Hmmm." I frowned at my black bodice with the silver clips. It pressed my tits upward and along with the black leatherlike pants did rather add some badassery. "Thank you? Better than naked, anyway."

"Only in that it keeps the wolfish orcs from grabbing your ass." Kragga had a sheathed dagger in hand. "This one, Datteo. Then we're off to lunch. Any recommendations, in the food department?"

"I was about to partake of a snack myself! The rat burgers from two stalls away are said to be good."

Was that rat burgers? Maybe the crab translator had it wrong? Must be.

Which was how we ended up sitting at the wharf on the edge of the concrete dock, munching on some suspicious burger-like creations. I had eyed the shop carefully, ready to bail if I caught sight of any rat tails. I lifted the lid on my burger, sniffed.

"Is something wrong?" Datteo had wriggled into place to my right, with his body almost sliding over the edge. The tentacles dangling below reached almost to the lapping sea. A blue, clear sea of gentle waves. This clarity of the water reassured me. Nothing could easily leap out and drag us in.

Kragga sat on my left, thigh to thigh with me. The contact warmed, and when I stared at his leg, and inhaled, I smelled my orc. Warmth turned to a heat then to a furnace that flared inside me and threatened to melt my thoughts.

Hurriedly, I returned my focus to the other side.

Datteo held a drink that he sipped, using a small tentacle.

"No burger?" I asked.

"No. Not my style."

"I am concerned about the meat used in this." I waved the suspicious thing.

"It's often not the usual meat. Supplies are low. We call them rat burgers."

Again, with that word. I grimaced and held the burger further away.

"It has no parasites and lives in the sea and in the ruins. I assure you it is tasty."

"Okay. Those are all pluses, I guess?" My stomach churned. Not a rat but the local equivalent. Supplies are low.

If this was a famine, again, I had done this.

Caught by a solid chunk of sadness in that moment, for it fell on me unexpectedly, I stared outward at the waves.

On the other side of Kragga, Doc Quinn tippy-tapped in on those robot legs. I listened without speaking as they discussed chemicals and alphas, omega reactions, and that he had a formulation he wished to trial. Kragga sounded noncommittal. I couldn't blame him for not wanting to be a guinea pig.

I studied my woeful burger and decided I would only eat the salad and the bun. A school of some sort of tiny fish had zipped past my feet and toward the shadows of the piers and the jetty. I drew out the meat, threw it like a frisbee, and it curved downward before it hit the water.

After the plop and small spout, it slid deeper.

Then it vanished as something dark unfolded from beneath the jetty, swallowed the meat, and retreated.

The sea had swirled at the spot, now it calmed.

I stared, not quite able to believe what I had seen. The fish were still there and happily zooming.

I nudged Kragga with my elbow. "Did you see that?" When he looked to me, I indicated.

"There? What did you see?"

"I'm not sure. Something ate my rat patty when I threw it there."

"I am not surprised."

"I guess." I kept frowning at the water. "What about that darkness beneath the jetty. Should someone check on that?"

"I am not going to dive in. Shadows tend to lurk in places where the sun fails to reach." He patted my leg. Though I was exasperated, the touch still stirred me, and my clit throbbed as if to say, there are more important things to do. I sighed and could not help but squeeze my thighs together to quell the sensations. That made it worse. Horny impulses were a pita. *Fuck that.*

Patronizing orc.

I knew what I had instantly suspected—that monster. Was this why orcs often followed Dark Lords full of evil? Due to a lack of planning and imagination?

I had a thought. "Did you say the monster dropped signs on people?"

"Yes."

"And they said?"

"The one that fell on Mog said *Help*, the other one said *Self-help Station*. A third sign found on its trail had *Shoe Sale Now On* written on it."

"Uh-huh." Ignore the sale? It seemed an anomaly. *Help self-help? Help me?* Could it be that? It could, of course it could. Or it might be random. I was sure Kragga would dismiss my theory.

Kragga went back to chatting with Quinn, so I turned to Datteo.

"What are you thinking?" He sipped from his drink with a slurp. Were his little eyes twinkling? If they were, it might be some gogogian trait, unless they put glitter in their eyes.

"I was wondering…"

"Yes?"

"About that tentacle creature that attacked Rishnak." Was that a huge eye looking out from under the jetty? I stared but could not be certain. "Could it be an alpha gogogian, turned by the singularity as were so many mauleons and orcs, which then made it grow larger?"

As in, large enough to fit under a jetty.

"That is doubtful. We gogogians don't really have a gender or a sex. We multiply rarely and in mysterious ways." He sucked on his drink while eyeing me. Somehow, I felt he was smiling enigmatically.

In other words, he wasn't saying how they reproduced.

I squirmed again and held my stomach. Something was making me feel queasy and itchy and horny all at once. Probably that burger.

I looked up at the sun and was struck by a question.

Although no one had told me it was so, a wisp of my wounded omega power had stretched out, unasked for, unsummoned, uncurling far above. It had felt for the sun, brushed by as lightly as a cloud. This sun was intimately linked to the engines of this starship. I could feel the twist and twine, the snicker and the flicker, as pieces of our existence were tortured by the WORSK engine.

Or was that my fantastical imagination?

I said in a whisper, "Who is driving the ship if everywhere is chaos?"

"That is a very good question." He slurped again, maiming the bubbles of his drink, unspeakably. "I do not know. Ask the mechlings or your Doctor Quinn?"

Then, just because I was feeling angsty, or annoyed, or ready to tempt fate again, though probably it was because I was a fool, I reached for the sun.

For a sliver of time, it faded into a simpering dull gray-yellow before blossoming again.

People around me gasped.

Shit. I still had it.

I didn't want it.

If I ignored it, this would go away. Right?

I shivered and felt both hot and cold, and wondered if I was coming down with an illness.

"Can we go back to the tower?" I grabbed Kragga's enormous biceps for comfort.

"Sure. Just give me a moment longer." He squeezed my hand.

12

KRAGGA

I woke to find myself with an enormous stiff erection and Char absent from our bed. This, after trying to fuck her properly last night and still being unable to get deep. The enlargement at the base of my cock was a reminder of yet another failure to knot. It wasn't just the remembered pain that annoyed me it was the *need*.

The need to get deep, plow her, and knot in her, dominated my thoughts.

I had allowed her in my bed for the first time, after many nights of her sleeping in the cage or on the floor beside me. Having her chained there and collared, at my beck and call, it was satisfying on a deeply… animal level.

She was not here, and the bed was cold.

I growled and stood, naked and already enraged. Where was she? The door was double padlocked and chained. There was only the balcony with the drop below that only mechlings would dare. I had no guard stationed outside the penthouse door because doing so seemed tantamount to admitting failure.

I would keep her safe and mine, and no one else would have that duty.

I do not like acting like an animal, I reminded myself, though my eyes when I glanced in the wall mirror looked red-rimmed, raw, and feral.

A growl was rumbling low in my chest as I stalked the rooms, searching.

"Charrrr. Where are you?"

Was that a meek call? I headed for the sound, and crossed the living room that stretched the length of the apartment. I only glanced out the glass that rendered a view out over Rishnak, to be certain she was not on the balcony.

She was not.

I wrenched open the door to my study, and there I found her, in my room of ancient books where my desk played king over the leftovers of past generations.

She had rearranged everything.

Books lay sprawled in heaps and piles, opened and exposed, or laid flat and open to show their pages to the floor. My desk with the research for the submission to Grut, the important submission for the mechlings, it lay on its side, with her inside the four legs and the table-top behind her and wedged against a bookshelf.

With great deliberation, I gathered the papers and the books and laid them beside the door.

Char was using my desk for a fort.

Crap. I knew what this was. She was nesting.

"Char." I sighed.

The female peeked at me from where she snuggled into the desk with some softer blankets, a rug, and pillows. Those had been found in other rooms.

"Hmmm."

She said nothing in return. I walked over, crouched, and stared. "You're nesting. It's an omega thing in preparation for mating." *Mating...* A drumbeat pulsed at my temples. I cleared my throat. "Are you okay?"

Char nodded.

No words. Which was unusual.

I could stay or I could go.

This nest was what an omega was supposed to need, and the alpha was supposed to wait to be invited in?

Fuck no.

I was not tramping down any pre-ordained path. I was not an animal.

"I will be back later."

She nodded and stayed partially hidden among the books, the rug, and the cushions.

Of all the things to use, she'd used my books. I caught myself snarling and was unsure why I did so, except it was not simply due to the desecration of my books. My reaction alarmed me. Backing away, I scrubbed my hand over my face, then paused with it covering my eyes so I could not see her.

"You're happy?" I lowered my hand.

She nodded again.

I was not succumbing to my lusts while in this mood. Yet leaving her here, free to go where she willed, seemed foolish. I fetched a padded manacle and some chain, then attached her to the heaviest thing I could find—a chest full of old weaponry that I dragged in, leaving scrape marks on the floor.

"Stay," I ordered her. I hefted the other object I had brought from the *jus-rak* chest. It had called to me, or so I justified this idea. I rolled the fuckspear, *madh gajol*, in my hand. This ancient device was used on difficult captives when other methods failed to cause sufficient acceptance.

It was this or the steel device.

Why the fuck not? I would be firm. I walked to her feet and tapped one with my boot. "Open your legs."

She hugged her pillows even tighter then did as I commanded, so that her see-through garment spread and gathered at the top of her thighs. The white night-dress was short, and I'd allowed her no panties or bra, for easy access.

My nostrils flared with craving for her.

I squatted and raised the fuckspear with the sea-blue, glass-like dildo at the end. The shaft was intricately carved with couples fucking. The creation of the dildo fused to the end was a formula lost to time.

This was a transparent substance that was close to indestructible, yet it gave like an erect cock. Cold but yielding.

I eyed between her legs and saw the shine of her juices around her well-displayed cunt.

"This is the orc *madh gajol* or big-cock fuckspear. We orcs have hilarious names, yes? I am going to insert this as far as it will go and tie it to you. Your duty is to fuck yourself and masturbate and then fuck yourself again." I bared my teeth. "If it isn't fully inserted when I return, I will make it so."

"Oh." Her eyes grew rounder.

"Perhaps it's best if I chain you." That was not a question. Already I was salivating.

There was something thrilling about restraining this female to my upturned desk while I did filthy things to her.

I fetched the necessary equipment, bound her left wrist to a stout leg of the desk, then tied her legs, splayed apart and to the desk structure to her left and right.

I stared at her, paced from side to side, stared again. *Fuckable and defenseless, and she is being so damn submissive.*

A fever swarmed me, making a maelstrom of my deviant thoughts.

I descended to one knee, with a thud when I hit floor.

Coolly, I inserted the tip of the glass dildo, revolving it, screwing it in, worming it higher. The tight stretch of her lips was obvious. When it would go no greater depth, I squeezed it in and out, a few times, enthralled.

Her squeaks and the wriggling of her ass as she tried to escape then tried to invite it inside... My throat dried.

The twist of her wrists in my bondage.

Her choked sighs, the wet noises, and the brazen swelling of her entrance.

I wrenched my desires loose from where she'd fastened them down and tied the fuckspear shaft to the crossbar that strengthened the legs of the desk. I wedged the spear against a book I nailed to the floor. Sacrilege to do that to a book yet also apt, considering.

She could pull the *madh gajol* further inside, but it could not be withdrawn.

I rose to my feet and stretched until my back cracked. Then I yawned as if this bored me. It did not bore me. My cock was iron-hard and digging into my pants as if to tear a hole to get at her.

It would wait.

Char had shut her eyes at my final thrust, but now she opened them and licked her lips. Her face was flushed, her breathing erratic.

"I think it best if you do not come. Imagine it is my cock impaling you, not this." I bumped the shaft of the *madh gajol* with my boot and she gasped. "But do not come."

Silent, she locked eyes with me.

Her leg muscles strained and flexed but she could not shift what I had done to her. This was such a perverted scene. I vowed to give myself some time before I came back, but when I did, I would sit before her and order her to show me how she had played with herself.

I needed to see her mess the floor with a pool of her own juices. I would make her grovel and beg.

Unable to resist one last touch, I kneeled again and pushed her night dress higher. Then I leaned over her belly and drew a trail with my tongue from her clit to her navel while she grew ever more distressed, while my hand wrapped over the dildo spear and pushed upon it.

I reamed her a little more, brought forth more reluctant noises from her throat.

Her mewls were music to an orc like me. An orc who wanted to knot in her and fill her with his hot seed. I sucked on her breast, chewed and sucked on her plump nipples until she was moaning and had grabbed at my shoulder with her free hand. My sweat made her hand slip.

Sweating? This morning was odd. I'd done so little, dragged a chest, tied her up, and my fingers shook and blurred in a strange haze.

I licked her one last time then shrugged her off me and rose again, eyeing this unsettled female.

"Fuck yourself. Do this for me. I will be aching for you when I come back, and it will not go well for you if you have disobeyed. Understand?"

"Yes."

She seemed pleased with the threat. Char was unusual. I recalled her love of spanking and of me making her ass red. Such a degenerate yet beautiful female.

I rescued the documents I needed that were, luckily, easily retrieved. Then I exited and descended in the elevator. I would see Quinn. We would sanely discuss personhood submission to Grut, and I would not growl at anyone. If he wished to do so, I would even discuss the alpha suppression drug.

I can control myself.

Rein it in. I am not unhinged.

I glowered, bleakly. My black orcs cringed as I stalked the lower corridors.

Fuck this. I was no mincing alpha obeying any sexual call from his omega when she wanted me. I was stronger than that. We orcs had always handled the rut. This would be no different from a rut. I would fuck her into the floor when I returned, and that was definitely, absolutely, *that*.

Only half-listening, I spoke to Quinn about mechling personhood, and he replied with talk about that and the drug he wanted to use on me because there was no other amiable orc nearby. It might help to quell the alpha impulses—the aggression, the rampant lusts, the impulsiveness.

I nodded, vaguely. "It's not of great interest to me.

His new face of sketched brown squiggles of hair and beard, large blue eyes, and spectacles, somehow looked perplexed.

He wandered away.

I drank more ale, counting the minutes until I returned to her.

Wait a bit longer. She will become flustered at my absence.

I threw some axes.

Throwing axes at my orcs was normal, I told myself, as I tossed back another shot of something that burned its way down to my gut. The splintering of the walls when the axes hit had been very satisfying.

The problem was, I could smell her down here, and her scent was getting stronger.

My snarl was fiercer than before, and the room fogged into a blur of reds.

I slid off the chair and stomped to the elevator.

Darglek. Remember him? Remember killing him?

My fucking subconscious was fucking with me.

And at the last second, I spun and reversed my steps. I focused on Quinn without doing more than curling my lip.

I wiped my mouth, snorted, blinked away much of the rage. "Give me some of that stuff. I'll be your experimental first."

Then I watched the needle go into my arm and sink through the flesh. The drug went through my veins. Ice sliding. It was a blanket in the middle of a blaze.

"Niiiice." I let my head roll back. I watched the far-away ceiling with the tattered chandeliers and wondered if I was better.

Doc Quinn retreated a distance, stayed there a while. I peered at him from under my brows.

"This." He tottered up and handed over a small bag that he pressed to my hand. "Another few doses. If it works, and I cannot tell yet if it does, once a week might be best, in the muscle tissue?"

"Aren't you supposed to inject it?" Could a mechling be afraid? I snatched the bag. "Fuck this. I'm going back to her."

13

CHAR

Having given up on touching myself because I was *this* close to climaxing, I sucked in a few breaths. My heart hammered as if it intended to break loose from my chest. I leaned back and banged my head on the underneath side of the desk. "Ouch." Accidental, but it hurt.

Without Him in the room, calmness had reigned, except for that one thing... except for feeling like a bomb simmered below in my pussy.

Okay, except for a few vital things. Firstly, of course, that fuckspear, the *madh gajol*, and secondly that I was tied to this desk, and that the fuckspear had been jammed up inside me to almost full depth. It squashed about when I tried to shift. Not that I could move much at all. I double-checked, as if in the last minute my hand might have been freed from the desk leg to my upper right—it was knotted so tightly I could not unpick it. Or my legs freed from those ties below?

Kragga had tied me securely, and I'd merely watched, happily. I rather loved bondage, just...

Eek. The other acts he perpetrated had been taboo-ish and weird and *omg HOT*. Though I was horny, which made me biased. Then he had left. The bastard orc had left. It was a sadistic sort of neglect.

Make yourself come.

I swore then leaned over to get a better look at the thing projecting obscenely from between my legs, as if a giant had decided to murder me by impaling me on his weapon.

"Fuck. If only." My pussy clamped down onto the hard device. Then I tried futilely to dislodge it, rocking to the side, shifting backward. That caused it to be dragged toward me because it was stuck up there. The straps wrapped about the fuckspear shaft, down near my ankles, grew taut.

Moving was a bad idea. It made me register the size even more intensely. My eyes were possibly bugging out. I rather liked being made to sit still for this but my existential bratty side made me want to give him the finger. It might tempt him to punish me, and he was already annoyed.

Damn. Did I even want to escape?

I shut my eyes to control my panting and felt my clit actually twitch. I had not thought it could do that.

"God." I groaned and looked down, hearing in my head his instructions to masturbate but not come. If I dared to touch myself, again, I would come so easily. I wouldn't be able to stop.

"Fuck this," I whispered. "Fuck this." I could see through the study's double door entry. The window looking out over the balcony called to me.

The world out there was minus fuckspears jammed into women just because their partners were felling ornery and horny.

He wanted to get up inside me further than ever.

I...

I wanted that, too.

Maybe I should obey?

I had wrecked the study, a bit, while making this nest. I guess I only had myself to blame for his ire.

Kragga angry had been something else.

Color caught my eye, drifting down outside the balcony window.

Flakes of gold, many tiny, flickering flakes of gold.

It was pretty and surreal. It brought to mind the beginning of a storm when thunder grumbled on the distant horizon.

Or the light sound of a violin playing in the night in a horror movie

The scratch of claws on a door at midnight when you didn't own a cat.

It was foreboding, though I wasn't sure why. An omen was waving its wee dark hand and saying: *Look. At. me.*

A wide dome of darkish blue ascended slowly from below the balcony, wider than the study doorway I looked through. It wasn't in here, at least. It was *just* outside the glass. I pressed my back into the desk's underside and held my breath as an eye hove into view. A big, bulky eye that stared at me.

Our gazes locked on each other. From somewhere to the right a tentacle sneaked in then plopped to the floor. It was inside the apartment.

It wriggled, snakelike, and moved nearer the doorway.

It had to be the creature from under the jetty. The creature that had smashed in downstairs and dropped signs on orcs. I had thought it might be an alpha gogogian.

I cringed.

The suckers on this blue tentacle were pink and somewhat cute, and that was so incongruous with a leviathan from the deep coming to rend me apart that I began to think.

Everything I had been told about the gogogians came back to me.

Friendly and lecherous.

Ancient and they loved to watch humanoids and trade.

Some thought they fed off emotions.

But they were never this big.

I chanced it. "Hello?"

Two wriggly tentacles advanced into the study. One raised itself while the second, larger tentacle flowed through the wide doorway.

If I was wrong, I was screwed.

"Hello back, human," boomed in soft tones thorough the door. The window glass rattled.

"What..." I gulped. "What do you want?"

"Help?"

"Are you a gogogian?"

"Yes."

"You've turned alpha, like the others? I think?"

"I understand. And thank you for seeing me and not running away."

"Uhhh." I studied my ropes. "That was the easy part."

"I want... you did ask what I wanted?"

"Yes." I blinked.

"Well. You see. We gogogians don't have sex, as you know it, and am confused."

"And?" I asked cautiously. Especially cautiously because the gold flakes were still falling, and I had realized they had zero to do with my visitor.

"My name is Radaka."

"Uh-huh." I wanted him to go away so I could think upon what the ominous flakes meant. My internal omega compass told me it had something to do with the sun. I wondered if anyone else could see them.

"Can I fuck you?"

"What? No!"

"I have novel desires. I know not how to satisfy them."

I bet. But no practicing on me. My mouth was open. I closed it. The tentacles advanced and reached my ankles then wriggled in place.

"Wait. Wait," I spluttered. "You have to ask for consent."

"Oh. I do?"

Which was when I heard the locks on the apartment door rattle and clank, and the door bang open.

I half expected a *fee fi fo fum* as Kragga tromped down the hallway toward us.

"You might want to hide," I told Radaka.

Too late, for Kragga skidded into view from the side, like in the movie *Risky Business*. His head turned as he followed the trail of the tentacle from the balcony to his boots, and from there to where the long, suckered appendage lolled and curled across the shaft of the *madh gajol* that speared between my legs.

Did his eyes spark with a fiery intense gleam? Hell to the yes.

"What is this?" That was a roar.

The axe in his hand silhouetted black, and the morning glare seemed to eat the edges. Flashes of gold floated down, as if the starship were quietly reminding me of priorities elsewhere. The single eye of the gogogian widened, and he flicked his focus from Kragga to me and back to Kragga.

"Oops," I mouthed. I was mortifyingly still turned on—dildo spear plus Kragga plus bondage made that unavoidable—only now, I was mildly fearful of the consequences of this mad scene.

14

KRAGGA

"It's a gogogian. An alpha gogogian called Radaka!" Char said urgently, still bound as I had left her, while I stood with my axe, Edogoth, dangling and turning slowly in my hand, heavy and deadly.

"Ahhh." Words failed me.

Gogogian? This one was a blue I recognized. The pink suckers clinched it. I rumbled, "Get away from her." It had barely left my teeth before my rage settled to the bottom of my mind, like silt in a frothing sea.

I had nearly raised Edogoth to sever a tentacle, or two.

Nearly, but I had not. Her keen blade would have cut through and wedged deep in the floor. I would have been obliged to yank to wrench her loose, while the sliced limb of the gogogian writhed and slapped and spewed its blood.

That would have been awful. I liked gogogians. I looked to the large, near-room-height eye of this one. It stared back, unblinking.

I frowned. I did not know the color of gogogian blood.

I did not sever the tentacle either. Instead, I stared. "And you are?"

"I am Radaka. I have… changed."

"Gone alpha, yes? You're big. Very big," I rubbed my stubbled, scarred chin, felt my tusks, and thought. Downstairs, my mind had been jumbled and fucked up. The last of my anger simmered and died. Instead, a perverted curiosity bobbed to the top. "Why this? What act do you seek to do to my human girl, Char?"

It seemed obvious but still.

My orc-human porn had, on the odd occasion, involved a tentacled creature.

The tentacles curled and pulled back, sliding over the fuckspear and away from Char, who sat befuddled, as if wondering what to do. Or, perhaps, what I would do. Tentacles halted at my feet. The tip of one and a few of its smaller suckers glued to my boot then unstuck themselves, as if they tasted me. I frowned at it.

"I am intrigued by sex," said Radaka. "Being alpha has caused strangeness-es. We do not usually not *do* sex."

"You can speak, yet you threw my orc, Mog, to the floor, and you threw signs."

"I did. At first I was confused and lacked speech."

"Huh. And now?"

"I am still confused." Radaka's small mouth tweaked upward, and the smaller face tendrils waved. "May I?" The larger tentacles returned to Char. "She told me to ask if I could fuck her."

My eyebrows rose.

"May you? What a good question." I walked into the room and up to her. "Have you obeyed me?" I figured I knew. The fuckspear had sunk no deeper. "Did you come? Did you push it in? I needed it, deep." I pushed on the end with my boot toe, as I had done earlier.

Char visibly swallowed. Signs of guilt or arousal?

"I tried and did not come. It has not moved? But this—" With her free hand, she pointed at the gogogian.

"Choose. I can use the steel dilator on you or a less harsh method."

I guided her to the outcome I wanted.

"Less harsh?" She nibbled on her lip and eyed the spear. "Yes."

"You are sure?" She nodded. I crouched before her to undo the straps on the spear and free her ankles.

Without hurrying, I extracted the spear. I didn't want to hurt her, and she was mine to toy with however I wanted to. The dildo end was dripping. A minor gush of leakage said this omega might be close to heat. "What do you think I mean to use instead of this?"

Her dress had slipped to gather at the join of her thighs. I pushed it higher, revealing her again, in a striptease show done to perfection.

"You don't get to hide," I growled softly.

She huffed and squirmed on her ass, as I smiled and pressed my fingers in a *V* to either side of her clit, dabbling in her moisture.

"I... *ummm*. I don't know?"

"But it's right in front of you, so I think you're pretending innocence."

"What do you mean?" But she glanced furtively over my shoulder, where our new friend would be obvious.

I pushed my hand lower, between her legs, massaging, circling her engorged and slippery entrance. At her sharp intake of breath, I cruised my hand further, meandering as far as her other hole, then I reversed the path of my fingers, to play elsewhere, in her cunt.

Slowly, I entered her, watching her telltale movements, soaking up her small noises. I wished I could trap all her cries and whimpers and wriggles in a bottle to remember this moment.

While she stared in disbelief and made those cute, strangled sounds, I fucked her harder, with ramming thrusts of my four fingers.

"There. That's it," I murmured, hovering my mouth at her ear and kissing her. Fingers in her and with her at my mercy, with the gogogian watching us. Just this once I would let him play with her. "I'd make you come, but I have other uses for you."

"Uses? Fuck. You don't mean..." Again she looked to Radaka. "You can't mean—"

"Can."

She was more relaxed than before but not enough to take me, sadly, not judging by where the *madh gajol* had stuck. And I needed in. I needed to knot in her. *Today*.

The imperative to do this was verging on an insane compulsion.

I. Needed.

Her jerky breathing when I brushed by her clit, then nestled my hand across her jaw with my thumb stuck in and fucking in her mouth, that told me what I needed to know. Turned on, already, and she knew my intent.

She knew. She fucking knew what I meant to make her take.

"You know what's coming, don't you? It's long and fat, and soft but hard, and perfectly formed for going into your needy cunt."

Again, she looked behind me, and she whined under my kisses.

"Exactly. After this, you will take all my cock."

Her pussy clamped onto my fingers, and more fluids flooded past them, dripping from my wrists, flowing wide on the floor. My pants grew wet at the knee. Yet not a word was said by her.

Behind us a tentacle slapped.

"He's waiting for you." I wedged my handover her neck, and firmly pinned her to the desk that had become a wall. Then I half-turned and said over my shoulder. "Come! I have a use for your big, juicy tentacles. You can learn what sex is now. Just this once, you may have my female, my Char." I extracted my cock from my pants. "Once she is reamed enough, I will be next."

Still, she was silent, only staring, her eyes wide, her heels digging into the floor. A tentacle went past my knee, making a rasping, slithery sound until it hit the pool of her wetness. There it slid silently, approaching her, between her legs, rising as if to see where to go.

Radaka had sent a good-sized one to take her.

"You can hear me?"

"I can," he replied.

The tip of the tentacle twitched and poked at her swollen lips, and Char whimpered. Such a pretty sound. I grinned.

"Be still, female. Do it! Fuck her with it, and I'll make sure she comes."

The tip touched her again, and the first sucker squelched inside, disappearing, worming in. More and more of the appendage working itself in, until it approached the girth of my cock.

Her pussy looked stuffed to fullness, and I slipped my thumb back into her open mouth.

"Good girl. Oh yeah, this is going to work."

With her tongue exploring and rolling over my thumb, she gasped at a final cram of the tentacle that made it buckle on the outside. Her eyes rolled up, and her back inched up and down the underside of the desk. Even more of the gogogian's member squeezed in.

"Enough!" I roared. "Now you must find a rhythm that gets her off." I wanted to get down there to suck on her, but there was no room.

How to be a sex coach and a filthy deviant all at once.

Radaka pulled out and rammed in.

The squelching noises amplified, and her wetness poured past the seal of tentacle and pussy. I leaned closer and began to stitch a path down her body—biting her skin, her neck, shoulder, her breasts, and nipples through the cloth. The threat of my teeth and no doubt the fucking, it made her bow upward. I massaged her clit. Her heels rhythmically pushed to the floor, making her arch even higher. Her free hand anchored into my arm, my shoulder, then found my tusk.

I laughed and pushed her down again. All the better to let a tentacle have her.

Her ragged breaths became choked moans.

Gogogians were supposed to register our emotions. This might blow his blue mind. The rut, the alpha desires were likely warping my morals. I did not care. A day ago, I would have asked her, but no longer, not now.

Not that I was letting him have her while she climaxed. Her orgasms were mine.

When it seemed she'd been used enough, forced open enough, I spoke.

"Out, Radaka!" I held her throat, and I smiled at her. I said the next while we locked our gazes on one another. My sadist was in full force. "You can tentacle fuck her ass while I take her from the front."

"Kragga, that's not possible." She put her small hand to my wrist but only held me lightly.

"It will be."

"You will destroy me."

"I won't." I kissed her hand but sent her a fierce glare. "I promise."

"Okay. Okay." Char panted and gulped. "Okay."

It was an answer I hadn't known I needed.

Radaka made a deep *hur-hur* noise I had never heard before. A dirty gogogian, what a shock.

"With pleasure. I'm enjoying the swamp of filthy passions streaming off of both of you."

The tentacle withdrew with an outpouring of omega fluids, and I moved over her and aimed my cock at her cunt and plunged in, with my spikes flaring automatically as I entered.

Her squeal made pre-cum squirt forth as I delivered the first ever full-depth thrust and nailed her to the desk, with a thud and a creak of timber, thank the fucking gods. Her bound hand clasped the strap like a lifeline. Her other hand clawed down my back leaving what must be a long and bloody scratch. She let out a mind-rending scream and jerked into an orgasm that crushed onto my dick and propelled me into the first-ever knot while inside her.

"Now, I have you," I tore the front of her night dress down the middle. When I thrust again, the desk splintered.

A second later, she squealed and tried to escape, and when I looked below, I knew why. A tentacle had found her ass, and Radaka was gradually feeding it in.

"Tighter hole!" He grunted enthusiastically. "And that orgasm... can you do it to her again? I *feeeel* those."

Char spluttered but seemed more into hanging onto my wrist than protesting.

"Yes." I was fascinated by *that* going inside while I still had her fully fucked and occupied by my monster of a phallus.

I plucked loose the tie on her hand, threw it aside. She wasn't going anywhere while being taken by both of us. Was this wrong? Did it matter? I coerced her. The thoughts bounced about in my head while she bounced on my cock, moaning, and drooling on my shoulder, leaving marks on my chest with her little teeth. My knot kept us firmly embedded and my thrusts were limited in their range.

She couldn't get away, but I doubt she wanted to.

The advantage of a tentacled partner? They could screw her in any position. I lifted Char and moved us to a wall where the bookshelves were absent and proceeded to fuck her brains out, just as I had warned I would.

Blue tentacles surrounded us in a surging, writhing cocoon as she succumbed to orgasm after orgasm, struggling nicely, and panting herself into a red-faced mess. My first *basja* injected into her and filled her, lending a squishy feel to being inside Char. My cock waded in come and omega juices, but as her body absorbed those liquids, the results of way too much sex, my arousal began to resurface.

Our desires had lessened, but I was not done yet.

Blearily, she raised her head and looked at me. I hugged her, and we slid to the floor.

"We are knotted. It makes you mine more than ever." I nibbled her ear lobe and the side of her neck, leaving more teeth marks and the redness from tusk scrapes. I rammed in a short distance to remind her I was here. Her thighs spread around me as she grunted at the pleasure, welcoming the impalement.

Blue tentacles surrounded us, swelling, pulsing, and a creature sighed heavily.

Radaka had crammed his body into the living room. His breaths were effervescent, as frothy as a windswept sea. "Do we ever have to end this? I could stay in her forever, fuck her, watch you both get off."

Oh fuck, was the gogogian high on sex?

Char rallied and looked at him, at the swathe of tentacles wriggling about us and across the books. "Houston…" she said softly, "we have a problem." She wrapped her legs around me, kissing my chest and trying to hook her feet at my back. She moaned quietly. "That feels so good. Let's not worry yet."

"No. It's time he left," I replied.

I had those other doses from Quinn. I could use them on Radaka. A tiny tentacle insinuated between us to caress her clit and suction over it while a second one started to feel its way around my balls.

The gogogian was definitely high on sex. Char was moaning louder.

By the time I had found an autoinjector in the package and injected it into Radaka, and then another two, and injected those also, just to be certain of the effect, Char had come yet again. It amused me to watch her do this.

It made me take her again, but with less force and more soft promises, more kisses, and quiet vows of love.

If that dose did not work, I was going to have problems.

Was it an hour and two climaxes later? Three? I lost track, but Radaka pulled from her, and his tentacles slithered away.

"I must go."

"Yes," I turned to watch as he withdrew from the room.

His voice echoed as he distanced himself. "I apologize for my insistence. Sorry, sorry... but it was so much fun."

"It was!" I agreed.

And he was gone. Polite as all gogogians were. The drug had worked, and I recognized the signs in myself of newborn calmness. Though perhaps that was because of other things, such as the female resting with my knot inside her.

And maybe I was lucky I had Doc Quinn to help me? My memory of Darglek's killing reminded me of that other horrible possibility. That was my lodestone, my path out of this. Do not become the orc my friend had.

Using gymnastics and puzzle-solving, I rearranged us so that she was before me and in my lap, without, thankfully, ripping my cock off at the base.

I must say sorry to the black orcs, tomorrow, for throwing those axes.

"The knot remains but not for much longer," I told my sleepy omega, holding her close with an arm wrapped over her.

"Mmm." She twisted then nuzzled my chest. "There is something urgent I must do, and I forget what it is."

"Later then. When this fucking knot goes. Plus, you owe me that secret." I shoved deeper, crossed both arms over her breasts to trap her. "Promise you will say."

"Okay. I will. Later, though." Her eyes were closing.

"Never again will I allow a gogogian inside you. That was too much." And I swallowed my orc pride and said to her what I had never said to any female. "I am sorry."

It was surely right to say this, except that one of her eyes opened to a sliver then wider, and she made a weird burbling huff. I leaned in... was that a purr?

And then she curled up with my knot in her and my hand brought to her lap. After some shuffling of her still-impaled rear, she raised my finger to her mouth.

And Char began to suck and nibble lightly on my finger.

My heart was hers from then on, and I wasn't sure why this was so. It just was.

I decided to settle this. "We are still not doing that again. No more tentacles in you."

She bit my finger hard and made a cute growl. After the shock of that, I smirked.

"Bratty human. We will see."

When at last the knot shrank and I slipped from her, disengaging, I made her drink water then enforced a shower for us both. It seemed essential, considering the fluids left pooling on the now disreputable floor in my poor study. After that, I had her put on a dress and took her to the rooftop, hand in hand, to where the ax-ramblers were parked. There we made a new nest of blankets and pillows, with added wine and food, as well as water.

The mock stars were out, as was the moon. I lay back, and Char nestled into the hollow of my shoulder and arm.

"There are many things we must discuss now."

"Oh. Yes." She wriggled lower into my body and draped her arm across my middle then added a muffled, "I guess."

"Hmmm. You will say now *what* your secret is or the spanking I deliver will echo and cause the toppling of towers."

"A spanking?" Her amusement was obvious in every syllable. "The perfect way to tempt me to defy you."

"Ahh, she recovers her tongue. So, it's to be a red ass until eternity?"

Char sighed. "No. I will say. And if you despise me and hate me, I will understand." Her tone was steeped in sadness. "I will say because there is no other way forward."

"Never will I despise or hate you." I hugged her. "Tell me. I forgive you, already."

15

CHAR

I forgive you already. His declaration only made me fear this more.

I did not know what would happen when I told Kragga of my role in the creation of the omegaverse and the partial destruction of this universe. It was too complicated, and I thought I had grown to love him, or at least bits of him... okay, definitely the bits that held his cock.

Considering my craving for being forced, and my need for kink on Earth, was it any wonder that a domineering orc would capture me in more ways than one?

The heart isn't just mysterious, it's stupid, or maybe it's actually wiser than I give it credit for? Kragga was a far deeper, more complex, and more loving creature than I'd thought possible. Maybe my heart was wiser than my head.

But, I pulled up my big girl panties—that I wasn't wearing because look ma, no underwear—I metaphorically yanked them up and told him what I had done while trapped on Vedrock's ship.

"I have had these powers ever since I became omega and then I decided to take my revenge on Vedrock..."

In silence, he listened to the whole story of how Vedrock had tortured me, how I had despaired and hoped to illogically level the playing field by making thousands more alphas and omegas.

How I knew I could bump the damage caused by the WORSK engines and make them tear and distort the 'verse.

And that doing this would cause some humanoids to turn omega or alpha.

What did I not know?

That it would create these crazed alphas, or that much of the galaxy would be plagued by riots and rebellions. That my actions would result in thousands, or tens of thousands, or maybe millions of deaths.

"And you made yourself go blind," he added, still trapping me in his immense arms, as if he thought I would run away.

"That, too."

"I am skeptical. You think you did all that? You seem kind of small and harmless."

"I did. I know it." I twisted my mouth. "I thought I'd lost my ability, but lately it has shown itself."

"How?" Again, there was a skeptical tone in his voice.

Which was when I recalled my conundrum with the falling golden flakes, and I peered outward and saw them tumbling past the dark backdrop of the buildings, though they were tinier than before and less noticeable. I'd thought those connected to the fake sun and the moon, and those were connected to the WORSK starship engine.

"I think, I can still do this." I raised one hand and made a twisting gesture. Not that I needed to, but showmanship works.

As always, there was a trepidation in me, both wishing to be capable, and praying for the reverse. Being powerless had its pluses.

The moon dimmed only to brighten as I lowered my hand.

"Oh. Fuck. Don't do that again. You can control the moon? This is... strange."

"I won't do it again." Then I laid my hand on his chest and waited for his reaction, because doing that had proved the rest of my story. It seemed unfair for this to happen now, but life loved making lemons. I would never have told Kragga if I did not trust him. "Now do you see?"

"I see that you *think* you unleashed a terrible power on the universe. That you broke everything across the galaxy by doing whatever it is you did? That's difficult to believe, even after you fucking dimmed the moon." He stared upward then took my hand and cradled it in his, turning it over and studying it, as if he could see some evidence there. "You did something bad, yes. I see that. For revenge, you say. You should have done *that* instead of *this*? Maybe? You didn't know these terrible things would happen. I see that, too."

I turned my hand into a fist, where it lay on his palm.

"You are going to have to give me some time to absorb this."

"Time. Okay." I was not sure why my wise heart had clenched in tightly, but it had. Was this the rejection I had feared?

"Time, yes. But there is this. We help to fix what has gone wrong, as much as we can, and I advise you to say nothing more about what you think you did, to anyone."

"Of course I won't." He still didn't believe me? Or he blamed me? I was frowning at what seemed a halfway choice. A noncommittal, let me ponder what you said. Did I want punishment for my bad deeds and not forgiveness?

Most of all, I wanted clarity.

I did not have it from this orc, and I'd just decided I was sort of in love? *Fuck.* I did not even have that forgiveness he had promised. I sniffed, tangled up in guilt and sorrow, and unsure I deserved anything from him anyway. "Okay. We move on."

As if he knew this was a good time to interrupt, Radaka climbed into view from below the edge of this garage level. His tentacles slid over the barrier in a lumpy blue tide, and he hauled up most of his body. The nearest ax-rambler was dwarfed. Blue tentacles sprawled across the floor.

Stunned and made uncomfortable by my memories of parts of him fucking me, intimately—as if there were any other way to fuck—I said nothing.

"I come to once more apologize, dear orc and human."

Kragga levered himself off the cushions into a higher sitting position. "We do not need a double apology, Radaka. Besides, I invited you in, before, in the room."

In? I was more than a little embarrassed, and my face heated.

"True, but nevertheless, I am at your service. I thank you for the invitation. I also wish to say, thank you for the use of your nethers, to your female, Char."

"Fuck," I whispered, hiding as much as possible on Kragga's chest.

He squeezed my arm. "You're welcome, she said. However, we two are resting. Is that all you need to say?"

"It is. Except that…" The gogogian looked down, past the railing and barrier. "I have attracted a mob of irate orcs at the bottom of this tower. Could you perhaps disperse them?"

Kragga sighed. "Very well. I'll be back."

He was still saying words to me, and that alone was a relief.

He slipped from beneath me, walked to the edge, then yelled in a voice that would carry, "Fuck off, you lot! This…" He pointed sideways using his whole arm. "Is a good guy! A gogogian made alpha. Okay?"

I thought I heard some cheers and shouting. They were nine stories down, though, so I might have imagined it.

"Fixed it!" Kragga told Radaka as he waved to those below.

Radaka bobbed his large blue head. "I thank you. I will go now." Already he was slipping tentacles off the building, and I figured he would be returning to the sea. "If you ever need my help, I am often near the jetty or beneath the small boats."

"Yes, I will remember. I thank you." Then Kragga returned to me, his hips swaggering in that arrogant male gait that never failed to attract me. He shook his head.

In the background, the gold particles floated down, taunting me. I needed to solve that puzzle.

"I think there might be something happening to the sun. I can see flashes of gold falling past, all across the sky." Could it mean something happened to the starship engine?

He stalled above me, his hands cradling the top of his head. "It can wait a night?"

"Perhaps. I don't know what it signifies." I shrugged, and he slipped back onto the rug but sat beside me. I missed his hands and knew he was creating distance between us.

"What can we do for the sun anyway?"

"I really do not know." *My love*, I had almost added that. "I just feel we should do something."

My love. That did not fit us anymore. Just like that, I'd driven a wedge between us, and it was no surprise. This was what I had feared. I would act normal, and maybe he would come back to me.

"That's vague." And he frowned.

A familiar tippy-tap on the hard floor warned of a mechling approaching.

"Doc Quinn!" Kragga said. "I'm beginning to wonder if I sent out accidental invitations. What can I do for you? You haven't redrawn your face?"

The doc lowered his chassis and scratched himself with a pincer arm, where an ear might be, if he had one of those. His head had sketched spectacles, brown wavy hair, and a scribbled-on beard.

"I like this drawing. However, to the task at hand. I hear the gogogian was alpha and yet on speaking to him on the way up here, I feel he has altered. There will be no more throwing of orcs?"

"No. I injected him with three of your doses. It worked. He was getting sex obsessed."

Thankfully, Kragga had kept the sex details out of this.

"Good! I have seen other data supporting that, coming through from other planets and places that tried this. The drug was effective on a gogogian? Truly blessed news!"

"Why are you here, doc? A new problem?"

"Yes. If we are to stop the hyper-alphas on this ship, we must put an aerosol of the drug into the air of the *Filthy Lucre*. To access that ventilation method, we must go to the mauleon side of the core and get permission to access larger quantities."

"Via Grut, of course. Okaaay." Kragga nodded sagely, though his fingers drummed on the rug beside me. "Anything else?"

"The submission on personhood to Grut?"

"The paperwork's done. But how to file it, or any other form, when Grut may be wrecked like the rest of the ship, and like the Grut Bureaucracy must be elsewhere in the galaxy?"

"The mechling network onboard ship tells me Grut lives. It functions, though it is limping along, in triplicate, as always. And this drug is being distributed on every planet and ship and satellite, wherever it can be done. They are wrestling the hyper-alphas to their knees." He click-clacked and waved several pincers moonward. "Access to Grut is also best achieved from the other side of the core."

"Because the tunnels are dangerous, and you have no fuel?" I asked, deciding to contribute to the discussion. I could see two problems and both of them said we had to be where Isolde was, where the mauleons lived on the other side.

"Yes," Kragga said.

I looked up. "To journey past the moon and the sun, and over the sea to the other side of the world. It sounds romantic." This was a welcome distraction from my own worries.

"Uhhh." The doc sounded nonplussed.

Kragga grunted. "Is it?"

Slowly, I climbed to my feet, untangled from the rug and cushions, and took a few steps, even as I heard Kragga rise and follow me.

I pointed above my head. "We must go there? Yes? Past the sun?" I turned to see both Kragga and the mechling nodding.

"But the ax-ramblers cannot jump, and the seas are too rough in the middle for oar-driven boats, and what *are* you thinking, female?" He eyed me from beneath those craggy, green orc brows. Then he advanced to stand before me. He raised his hands as if to touch me then let them fall. "Well?"

At least he was close and talking to me.

"Radaka, the alpha gogogian…" I quirked my mouth, hoping this did not sound stupid. "Our friend. He is huge and can swim. Could he tow the boats to the other side, with orcs and mechlings in them?"

Where I could see Isolde for the first time since the day we were abducted by aliens and put in a holding cell, to wait for our owners to claim us. My mind had butted in and dragged me down to a grim reality.

Fuck reality when it was being grim. I wished, though, that I could put my hands in Kragga's, to be comforted by his solid presence.

"Ahhh. Hmmm." He tilted his head side to side, thinking. "That sounds—"

"Like destiny?" I suggested.

"Doable!" Doc Quinn nudged his head between us at chest level. "I will communicate with the gogogian and the mechlings on the other side. I will tell them to prepare for our arrival."

Then he scurried off and vanished over the side.

Kragga still had his mouth open. Slowly he closed it and studied me.

"Thank you, for your thoughts."

And that was that. We packed up the gear and moved below.

16

CHAR

The orcs decided they needed a list, a manifesto of what must be done in the coming days. I volunteered to record it. Kragga agreed.

It meant I spent time writing it out, down in the lobby of the tower, because they all had suggestions—from Doc Quinn and the gogogians, to the orcs themselves. Kragga mostly sat on his throne, looking grim.

I assumed this was a good reason to avoid being alone with me in the room.

Time. He was taking a lot of that.

I was happy to compose that list and put off discussing things with him, coward that I was.

Once the list was finalized, drawn up, and signed, and that was so weird, having to get it signed… it only took the orcs a few days to organize an amphibious invasion of the other side. Raucous, as they often were, yelling and brandishing things and drinking, they packed weapons and axes, food, and useless things I was sure this invasion of their own ship did not need.

They had easily convinced Radaka to ferry us over by hauling some small boats that normally used motors. Doc Quinn contacted mechlings elsewhere on *Filthy Lucre*, and did whatever he needed to do to get the alpha-calming drug gathered or the manufacture hastened.

At last, we were ready. With axes underfoot and strapped on, with holstered pistols and laz rifles, with our hands clenched on anchor chains, hawsers, gunwales, and whatever the other parts of the boats were called, we set off.

The bows of our small armada plunged recklessly into the sea, flinging spray. Sinking seemed highly probable, and those weapons would drag them straight to the bottom. It looked like a drunken party of armed college students that had hijacked a kraken to go surfing.

We should have had trumpets playing, or an orchestra, as we skipped across the surface leaving churned white water in our wake. This was how the Vikings must have looked when invading England.

Next time, I promised myself, put orchestral music on the list.

Gripping the tow ropes in his tentacles, Radaka swam us toward the mauleon side. The long hair of the orcs streamed backward, froth from the waves spattered us, and the fish beneath looked surprised and dashed away. In places, the water in this artificial sea was clear enough to let me glimpse the denizens beneath. The fish seemed out of place, and so did the red seaweed that floated by.

A few orcs threw up, and some appeared to turn a green that was greener than even an orc should be.

The irony.

These orcs traveled on starships that attained speeds that blistered the asteroids they passed, speeds that screwed over the space-time continuum. However, trapped inside a starship hull, it was impossible to see the results of their speed. On the surface of an ocean, it was obvious.

Even Kragga seemed bothered.

I clutched Kragga's hand. He pretended not to see my neediness. The rigidity of his stance throughout the entire two-hour journey, and his silence, told me either boats were not his thing, or I was not.

I was his omega, he had said. I wrinkled my forehead and tried to not weep.

I must remember there was more to my world than Kragga.

Isolde, I'm coming. I hadn't exchanged a single word with her, or an image, and yet we had been so close to each other. It was entirely possible she had been killed.

"I hope Isolde is okay," I murmured as we approached a shoreline.

"Your friend?" Kragga coughed and relinquished his death grip on the anchor chain. "I hope so, too. Gideon would take care of her. I should have asked Quinn for news."

My heart skipped and did a short dance. We were conversing. *Play it cool, calm, collected.*

"I didn't know you could?"

"The awoken mechlings follow her sword, Smorg, and the smartass weapon goes everywhere with her and Gideon, last I saw them."

The talking sword—I had heard rumors of this weapon and had wondered if these aliens had watched too much Conan. I'd been informed it could talk due to programming embedded in the hilt. A sword still seemed a total anachronism. Then I remembered the axes and almost eyerolled at myself. Silly me.

At sight of a long sandy beach, Radaka slowed, then crawled into the sand, his tentacles pulling him forward, as well as the ropes he held. The boats were swept onto the sand by momentum, and ours ground to a halt, with sand crunching beneath the hull.

In a long, crooked line, the orcs advanced up the beach. The only sign of the disturbances, so far, had been a few dead humans floating in the middle of the sea.

The narrow section of sand gave way to pebbles then, as we topped a small rise, small houses came into view. An opposing line of… aliens confronted us. I knew them all by now, the alien species, and my crab translator knew all the languages. Yet they were aliens. I'd become used to the orcs.

Hoping against all the rickety odds on this stupid starship, I picked through the crowd, looking from one to the next, as they rushed toward us.

Welcomes and shouts of glee rang out.

"There!" I pointed and showed Kragga who had stopped alongside me. Her flamboyant red hair stood out, as did her shortness. "Isolde!"

I ran to her, arms out, dodging the others as they whacked each other's backs or shook hands. We skidded to a halt before one another, panting, laughing, and I grabbed her in a hug and screamed a few times.

"We're both okay! We're both okay," she said, wiping at her eyes with the hand I wasn't grasping.

"Yes." I wasn't telling her I'd gone blind and had been tortured, though she was sure to notice my eyes, because she had almost certainly been through hell to get to this day. And then she did notice. Her flinch was obvious.

"Your eyes are the wrong colors, and different. What happened, Charlotte?"

I shook my head. "Another time, maybe. For now, let's be thankful."

We smiled at each other, though there was a hint of regret in her smile. Mine would surely also reflect the memories our meeting had triggered.

Her gaze flicked to my side then upward, as she saw Kragga returning from greeting another orc. "I remember you. Kragga?"

"Yes, this is Kragga." I grabbed his big arm, grateful for his silence, for letting me pretend all was fine between us. "I guess I should call him—" I hesitated to say what would have been an embarrassing error. I was such a dumb ass. Then he casually fastened his hand at my nape and shook my neck, though without much force.

"Your friend is mine now, Isolde. As you are Gideon's."

Fuck, he'd claimed me.

Also, fuck, what did this actually mean? I was rather lost.

It was a blatant summary of ownership but nothing more.

Isolde hugged me again and whispered, "It's okay."

I breathed, calmed, tried to center myself. "I'm omega, and so are you. Yes?"

What if he claimed me yet hated what I had done? Maybe even hated me? I eyed him and found nothing in his stonelike expression to change my opinion on this.

Orcs tended not to be emotional, though, unless there was battle, drinking, or sex involved.

"Yes." Isolde looked about. "We should talk more when we are settled. Things were unsafe here for a while. A lot of humans and some mauleons went aggressively alpha. Some were killed. Some grew twice as big."

I nodded. "That tentacled creature who pulled all the boats." I raised my eyebrows. "He is a gogogian alpha."

"I saw that. Charlotte, let me find Gideon and introduce you."

I had met him before, I realized as we closed in on a circle of black orcs and a few mauleons.

This was the gold-maned mauleon who had abducted us from Earth. He was taller than most of the other mauleons, more muscular. The alpha effect, of course. Seeing him brought back harrowing memories.

I did wonder why so few orcs had become aggressive alphas. A genetic difference, I guessed. What I had done, unleashing waves of singularities at once, would be to blame for the worst effects. It had created some sort of double whammy that made some alphas turn into true monsters.

As we followed our greeting party back to an area they said was safest, we came across evidence of the fighting. Laser scars on buildings. Completely burnt-out shells of houses. There was only one body, which they carried away, but none of this damage was new.

"It's taken days to bring things into order again." Isolde had seen my distress.

"Yes. We could see the fires from Rishnak."

"Let's move on." She took my hand again, unaware that I was the cause of this. How could I ever tell her? I'd told Kragga because it had seemed right, and he had insisted. And look what that had done. Telling Isolde might kill our friendship. I was not sure that I, as in my former self, would even want to know me.

The day took on a somber tone that dulled the better parts of it.

Isolde pulled my hand, and I trailed after her. We were surrounded by huge aliens, and every so often they switched back in my mind into the beasts I had seen them as, on the night we were taken. Knowledge and experience had jaded me, but not enough. Who was the bad guy here? All of them? Or was it me more than anyone?

They gave us places to rest and fed us, then took us to a venue called the Blood and Guts Tavern, where preserved beast heads were mounted on the walls, along with what looked to be an anti-aircraft cannon from WW2. As we weaved through the patrons, I banged my head on a horn sticking out from the wall and swore.

The Blood and Guts name was appropriate, considering the crowd was a bunch of weapon-carrying orcs and mauleons. There were some aliens who appeared more of a human type, and though most were armed, it wasn't all axes and swords. Whatever the sleek alien pistols and the laz rifle weapons could do, I was certain they could kill.

Did orcs love axes for their ferocity, their deadly appearance, or because firing projectile weapons inside a starship was bad news? If this were a dragon fossil in which we resided, surely a few bullets would make little difference to the integrity of the ship?

The tavern grew crowded, though few were drinking beer or wine or any other liquor, judging by the scarcity of glasses set out on the tables. They were waiting for something.

Gideon and another alien, of a race with furry ratlike noses, rose before the assembly in this widest room of this pub. Gideon banged on the table before them. His mane swished across his shoulders as he surveyed the throng. "Quiet! I am Gideon, as most of you know. This is Laskar, the captain of *Burning Chaos*."

When the talking lessened and the crowd had stopped fidgeting, the rat alien, Laskar, spoke, "We are here to hear from the orcs what must be done to finally quell this uprising of the alphas. We have had enough of killing and fighting our own people! This!" He held up and shook the sheaf of papers that was the Orcish Manifesto I'd written in Rishnak City. "This is what we will do! And so, I invite the author of this, a human female called Char-lotte—"

"Now called only Char!" bellowed Kragga, loud enough to deafen me if I wasn't already struck dumb and mortified. "This is her." He pointed at me.

"Char, the mate of Kragga, will come up here and explain the list." Then he waved to us. I would be towing Kragga, if I had to do this.

I grabbed his hand.

"Come with me."

Grunting at my insistence, he let me drag him through the people.

Maybe there was hope for us? I had to get him to talk some more, but later, after this public display of whatever—my writing? I wasn't sure why they wanted me to read. I squashed the little gremlins of anxiety worming about in my mind and stomach. Later, much later I would regain my courage, sit with Kragga, and talk.

"Here they are! Give them a hand." Gideon gestured at us. "Please! Inform us so we can get the fuck back to normal."

Oh my. I did not think that was ever likely. Not since the day I created the omegaverse was anything going to be normal.

We must fix what we can, Kragga had said. *Okay. Fine.*

I drew a breath, ignored all the eyes staring at me and my quaking knees, and I began to read the manifesto.

"One. Gain permission F942A from Grut and get access to storage depot number…"

17

CHAR

The elevator opened with an almost inaudible *swoosh* that would have been at home on Earth. The outer controls reminded me of home, too. I swept aside my petty nostalgia for elevators and followed the small army into the corridors. More people emerged, all armed, all cautious, from the adjacent elevators.

Although fuel was scarce, the elevator system was powered by the ship. Which was nice, convenient, and had not made me nervous in the slightest. *Ugh.* I hated the idea of being stuck in an elevator on a starship that was not looking at its best. It would possibly require a form 900A432 sent to Grut to get oneself freed, on the *Filthy Lucre*. How did anything ever get done?

Tramping through the ship corridors and stairways on foot to reach the Grut offices would have taken days, though.

"Come. Keep up." Kragga nudged my arm, and I smiled and nodded, then resumed walking at his side.

The weapons being flourished by the fifty or more warriors made spiky belligerent shadows on the lefthand wall. It was an evil-themed montage—watching the people move then seeing those pointy shadows. I shuddered. My imagination was doing overtime.

Simply getting to this point, to the corridors that led to Grut, had meant hard fighting.

Two dead alphas lay in our wake, staining the floor with their blood. Several of our team wore bandages. Doc Quinn and some other mechlings had traveled to near the necessary supply depots. Our job was to get permission to open them. The Grut Bureaucracy held the reins for most things on the *Filthy Lucre*, as well as elsewhere in the galaxy, or so I'd been told.

Want a truckload of apples? Ask Grut. More drugs? Ask Grut. The alternative was to bash open doors, and this place was made of solid rock and metal.

Isolde kept close to Gideon, her mauleon, and to Smorg. The snarky sword was at her heels in the hands… pincer hand, of a hip-height mechling with green fur and googly eyes. A furry cushion on legs with a sword was how I'd described him.

Isolde had laughed.

"Here." Kragga showed me his comm and the map on the screen. "Up ahead. We go left at that T-junction."

"Okay." There had been fighting here, too.

As we turned left, I noted chunks missing from the walls, stains, a hole in the ceiling, and none of it was repaired—though there were little labels. An orc waited with his back to the wall beside the white door we needed. *WSG101* was emblazoned on it in red alien text.

He waved us down, and the ten or so aliens and mechlings accompanying our detail crouched. They trained their guns at the door.

The orc stepped out, then turned, twisted the door handle, and kicked open the door. He froze as he scanned the interior. "All good. You can go in."

Four of us entered. Five, if you counted Smorg.

"That was fun!" Smorg said, as I passed the mechling wielding him. "Can you do it again but with more style? And you might consider shooting something."

"Shhh," Isolde admonished him.

Bemused, I entered the Grut Bureaucracy office. In here, the walls bore the same sort of damage we'd encountered outside. I peered at the labels stuck next to the marks. A reference number was written on each one, in tiny text. *Damage 6799901* was printed on the nearest one. I laughed and shook my head.

Kragga scowled but seemed to understand when he, too, looked.

Humor makes the world go round. Talking made the world make sense, though. I understood why he found it difficult to discuss what I'd done. Even I still thought it was appalling as well as bizarre.

Next time I did something awful I would scale it down… like I could forget to pay the rent or use his toothbrush? Or if I were daring, get rust on his axe. Nuking the universe was difficult to forgive.

And maybe, just maybe, he had personal reasons to hate what had happened? How many orcs had died over this alpha-omega situation? How many of his friends? I should ask him. I should be brave and ask him.

A few meters away in this stark room, a male clerk sat on a metal chair before a computer screen. Sweat was rolling down his temples and forehead and sticking his black curls to his skin. But he leaned back and asked formally, "What can I help you with?"

"These." Gideon propped his laz rifle against the desk then handed him the two forms we were presenting. The personhood one was processed first, and the clerk made no comment over the chances of it being passed.

The form for opening three supply rooms, he stamped those and printed something on them, then he placed them in a pile to his right after entering something on the screen. The ventilation systems and other request forms were being handled by our other teams.

"*Uhh.*" Gideon shifted his feet and his long brown coat swayed. "What's happening with that last form?"

Isolde smiled at the clerk. "We need that approved ASAP, please."

"Oh! Sorry. It's approved, but it's all useless. By the time you get to those depots, the ship will be entering a black hole that is going to swallow us forever. It will turn us into a chunk this big." He held up his finger and thumb to show the tiny size. "Look."

He pressed something and swung the screen. Big letters scrolled down it.

WARNING. PUT YOUR AFFAIRS IN ORDER.
THIS STARSHIP WILL DESTROYED TODAY DUE TO STEERING PROBLEMS.

Beneath that was a count-down timer.

"Steering problems. What? How is that going to do *that*? And when did you find this out?" Gideon drawled.

"When I started my shift."

"Fuck."

I wasn't sure who had said that, since I was more than a little rocked. It may have been Kragga.

"What can we do to stop this? And why is it happening?" Isolde leaned in and tapped the guy on the forehead.

Smorg gave a static-laden sigh as the mechling held him higher. "Typical. Is there a form to fix this?"

"No form. Sorry. I wish there was one." He stared helplessly at his desk before adding, "The command deck was apparently taken over by an alpha. They are all dead because he became enraged and ran amok. Over two hundred crew were in there. We only know this because we were sent data from other ships tracking our path. That told us what our ship is doing, then the internal data was checked and… some footage of the command deck was accessed. The ship has been moving at an unsafe speed for days."

Now, finally, I understood what the golden flakes that came off the sun and moon were telling me. The WORSK engine was overloaded and possibly self-destructing.

"Is there no one who can get into that command deck and steer us aside and slow us down?" Kragga asked, pulling me with him as he advanced.

Two hundred dead. It would be a gruesome place to walk into, especially days after they died. I shuddered.

"No. We cannot get through the door. And no mechlings are allowed inside. It's not unlockable by anyone here. Getting permission for entry will take days, though my superior has initiated that request. It was set this way for security purposes."

Gideon picked up his laz rifle and gripped Isolde's hand. "Maybe we should grab our biggest weaponry and try forcing our way in?"

"You could?" The clerk opened his hands. "I don't know if anything will work. I really wish I did know something."

I knew something that might work, except the last time I did something similar, I'd fucked up. This time... what was there to lose? We would die anyway.

Gideon turned to us. "I'm doing this. If you want to try, follow me. You can stay," he commanded Isolde.

"As if that would help anyone, Gideon. I'm coming with you."

He ran out the door, and we followed. I had to since Kragga was still towing me. After gathering everyone he could talk into this, Gideon set off jogging.

"To the elevators. Meet you all at the command deck entry!"

With a roar and the usual shaking of whatever they carried, orcs and mauleons and the few humans, as well as the rat-faced captain, trotted off toward the elevators.

Which was when I aimed to tell Kragga I had to stay to try my own weird solution to this. Instead, I found he had already stopped dead.

He barricaded me against the wall, propping his arms to either side while glowering. "Well? Miss Char? I saw how you hesitated and that look. I know you well. You have an idea that's to do with..." He huffed and glowered some more. "Your powers?"

"Uh. Well. Yes? But it's power, singular."

"Does that matter?"

I shook my head.

"I've been an ass, haven't I? But there is no time for this, for me saying more of those fucking sorries. What do you need from me? I accept that you actually may have caused this plight, this catastrophe of sorts that has plowed through the universe, but you did not mean to do this." He bowed his head and shut his eyes. The lines on his face deepened. "If it was not for the fact that we will die anyway, I would not say this, would not ask it of you." He raised his head and looked at me. "But we are going to. No matter how much I want to keep you safe... What do you need?"

I was shocked. Also that was an exceptionally long, almost-apology from this orc. What did I need? I clasped his arm, slid my hand up to those wicked spikes I must avoid when hugging him. I crept my fingers between them, happy that we had resolved this.

"Thank you for telling me. The first bit."

Kragga harrumphed but took my other hand and kissed my palm, then closed his fingers over mine.

This was the good part before the storm hit us, before the black hole swallowed us, and I would treasure it.

"I need somewhere quiet. Somewhere I'm not interrupted?"

"Here then?"

At which moment a Grut employee rounded the T-junction intersection and trundled past with a trolley on wheels. We waited for him to open a door and go in.

"Not here then." Kragga frowned. "I think I know where. There is no large hall or anything, but... follow me."

Again he took my hand and strode off, making me jog to catch up. "Where is this?"

Instead of entering any of the elevators, he went right along the face of them, then we headed up a different corridor.

"You'll see. While we walk though, I have questions. If you do this, if you can stop the WORSK engine..." He paused and looked at me. "And is that your plan?"

"To slow it, yes. Stopping it would, from what I've seen here, maybe stop a lot more things on board—elevators, lighting, air purifiers, heating, gravity?"

"Huh. I hadn't thought of that, but yes, it would. Come." Up ahead was an illuminated door. "If we survived that, and somehow the *Filthy Lucre* is steered away from this black hole, what will everyone do to you? You may as well put up a sign saying, 'look at me, guess what else I did before this?'"

Like the rest of the corridor, the illuminated door was white, but written on it was the alien equivalent of *Restroom Facilities*. "Why here?" I gestured at the door.

"It's biggish in area, quiet? And private if you toss everyone out. My question, Char? What will we do?"

"We?" I had to know, though he had been clear. I needed those words said.

He sighed and rubbed his face. "Yes. We are together. I have already forgiven you. Twice now. I'm over being an ass."

"An orc ass?" I hadn't been able to stop myself saying that. I didn't know why, but it made this funny for all of one second. "Sorry." But I grinned. He was back and said he'd never left me, in spite of the silences and the grimness. "Thank you for the forgivenesses."

Kragga actually eyerolled, then he smacked on the door, opening it, and bellowed. "Anyone in there?"

Silence filled the corridor.

"Good. Think about what I said."

About not being vilified if I did this? "If we survive and all that, how can I avoid that?"

He mimed zipping his lips. "Now get in there. I'll guard the door. None shall enter. Is that right?"

I thought hard. "None shall pass?"

"Yes." He grinned. "I always wanted to be the good guy like Gandalf. Do not make yourself blind again or hurt, or anything. I cannot bear to lose you to this, not after I asked you to do it. Take care." He pulled me to him for a fast, rough kiss then stepped back and unsheathed his axe. He waved me in like a doorman at a hotel.

The door closed.

We were kissing again. I smiled and put my hand to my mouth, remembering his touch, his taste. Remembering everything about him, really.

It was my choice anyway, I had wanted to say.

I was pretty sure that quote was not from the good guy, because it wasn't Gandalf, and it certainly wasn't *LOTR*. It would be kinder not to tell him.

It was the thought that counted, and Kragga was a good orc. The best kind.

"Now. Let's see." Nervously, I surveyed the empty restroom stalls and the sinks. "I cannot steer this ship. I know this. All I can do is try to slow down the WORSK engine on this starship, when I'm miles from the controls and standing in a bathroom."

I had wrecked the galaxy from further away.

And then, if we survived that, I would have to avoid the pitchforks and the tar and feathering afterward.

"Simple," I told myself, raising my arms dramatically, because it really couldn't hurt and maybe the universe liked theatrics?

I listened to my heartbeats. *On the count of ten.*

Nine. Eight. Seven.

I didn't know what I was doing, and no one could help me.

Six.

If this turned out the way my last efforts did, the WORSK engine might explode.

Five.

I don't want anyone else dying.

Four. Three. Two.

Please?

One.

18

KRAGGA

I turned my back on the door to the restroom, grounded the butt end of my axe on the floor, loosened my pistol in the holster, then I waited.

"None shall pass."

I was still smiling at that when an announcement was made through a speaker system I never knew we had.

"Warning to all residents, lifeforms, and other aliens on board the Filthy Lucre. *We are making this warning after Grut formally agreed to an emergency usage.*

"The ship is about to crash into an anomaly known as Black Hole 331900B. In doing so, we will all die and be crushed into a tiny ball of squashed atoms. We advise you make your peace with—"

A mild ultrasonic ringing began. A white light seeped out from under my feet. It was the restroom door. The ship itself seemed to shiver. The white light, which had to be really fucking white to show in this undamaged corridor, blew out in a flare that seemed ready to take the door off its hinges then ran all the way around the edges.

The corridor was dazzling enough to be blinding, and I shielded my face with one hand. I left it there until the light slowly dimmed and vanished. The ship ceased to tremble and ring. The door made a *thunk* noise.

I shook my head, blinking, and I stared at where the door must be until my sight returned.

Was that it? Should I go in?

I dithered, waiting, not wishing to interrupt what Char might be doing, but I was hurting because *she* might be hurting.

The speaker started up again.

"This warning is now canceled. The ship has slowed sufficiently. Statistical rendering of the situation shows there is enough time for repairs to take place, once all the bodies are removed from the command deck, and we have permission to enter. If you have any relatives involved in the command structure of **Filthy Lucre**, our condolences are offered. Use Form DED404 to apply to collect your relatives. Thank you for listening."

The damage to her eyes that last time, the red web around them and her almost dying, it made me hesitate, but going in was inevitable.

This was like charging into battle.

I barged through the door, and directly before me Char lay sprawled on the floor, facedown.

"Char?" I skidded to a halt beside her on my knees and turned her over. Though she moaned and seemed unconscious, her eyelids and around them appeared fine. But of course they should be—these were synth eyes. "Char?" I whispered, swiping away hair from her face.

Her eyelids opened and those violet and yellow eyes—orc yellow, I decided—focused on me. Her hand crept up and held her stomach.

"Kragga, did I do anything good?"

"You did, Charlotte, you did."

"My real name?"

"Temporary." I smiled. "Just testing your brain power."

"Oh. Well." She looked down, along her body. "My stomach hurts and you… you're on your knees. So, you've fallen for me, finally?"

That her stomach hurt seemed a warning sign. I clambered to my feet, carefully, with her in my arms. "We need to find a doc."

"*Shhh*. Important things first. You like me?"

I laughed and headed for the door. "Absolutely. I forgave you, but do you forgive me for not believing you, for blaming you even though I didn't quite believe?"

"Complicated." But she returned my smile and tugged on one of the dangling tails of hair I had gathered with a metal clasp. "I forgive you, if you kiss me."

Which was why, when I hooked open the door with my boot and went out into the corridor backward, we were deep in a drawn-out kiss.

"Halloooo! Lean back so I get a better view?"

Smorg the sword was out here, with his mechling carrier cushion, waiting for us.

We stopped the kiss and stared. I hefted her into a better position in my arms, then Char clutched her stomach again and winced.

"There has to be a reason for that. Doctor. *Now*. Smorg, out of the way."

"Wait, before you go. I'm here because the mechlings tell me that they backward-extrapolated the data from the singularity explosions that caused the hyper-alphas and the new omegas. This began on the ship she came from. Vedrock's ship, the *Social Deviance*."

That was shocking. What could we do? Run? Now that the starship had slowed, one of the merc ships could be launched, such as our *Burning Chaos*. But… there were many obstacles.

"You can't prove anything." I bared my teeth at Smorg.

"No, not until the event that happened here. Never fear. I'm getting that door replaced and the footage of this corridor is erased. I like being alive. You can kiss my sexy butt later. Shoo!"

"The door? What do you mean fixed?" I swung and saw the door had crumpled at the edges. "Fuck. Smorg…" I eyed the sword. It was still weird talking to this demonically snarky piece of useless tech. "Thank you."

Char was too busy curling over in pain to say anything. I started to run. "Contact a doc for me?"

"Okay! We're coming though. Your comm is useless, and I can use the mechling network. Hurry, mister orc!"

Hurry? I muttered swear words and bumped the elevator control with my knee.

Smorg and his friend sidled inside with us.

Balefully, I eyed him. "We're good?"

"More than good. My sword-ish lips are melted shut. Though not really. I need to chat, so I can instruct you when to kiss my butt. The hospital at 16Z is functioning and awaiting you."

I grunted and held my tongue.

Char rallied and smirked at me, though her forehead creased with pain. "Doctor, STAT, please, before you do something bad to that sword."

I was still muttering when I ran into the hospital on the lower level.

Once we had a bed in an examination room and a female humanoid doc was scanning Char's belly, I'd simmered down.

"You're an alpha, sir, and she is omega. You should have told us." The doctor seemed fidgety and anxious.

I understood why. I adjusted my chair to be nearer the bed. "I should have warned you, yes."

She tilted the screen so both of us could look.

"Omegas, we do extra security for those. However." She indicated a blur on the screen. "There is some internal bleeding and damage, though of no obvious cause. It's puzzling but should be healable, especially in an omega." She looked at Char, where she'd propped herself up on her elbow on the bed. "A day here, and she can go."

"Thank the gods." I twined my fingers in Char's hair. "The painkillers are working?"

She nodded. "Being away from Smorg helps, though he was a good guy, too."

"Hmmm. I suppose. Yes, he was. He knows you're amazing, same as I do." She had singlehandedly, almost, saved this ship.

Char shushed me and frowned.

We would not be telling anyone, though. Ever. As long as Smorg and the mechlings stayed silent, we could weather this.

"Never again. Ever." I kissed her knuckles.

"One other thing," the doctor said. "Your omega is coming into heat again. In a week, perhaps. You might want to be prepared. It's another good reason to leave the hospital."

Then she smiled at Char, as if my female was a strange new specimen she did not quite know how to handle.

In heat? I knew exactly how to handle that, and how to handle Char, and I was beginning to understand the changes in her scent. "Thank you, doctor."

19

CHAR

Once the drug was aerosolized and the hyper-aggressive alphas had calmed, everything had settled back to close to normal—or so I was told. I'd never seen much of *Filthy Lucre* when it was normal. I'd seen a holding cell, and Grut offices, and then I'd been transported to Vedrock's ship. How strange it was to find myself one of the residents.

Looking at Viewport One from my upside-down position, while draped over Kragga's shoulder, was interesting. Traditional entry he'd said, smacking my butt lightly and growling. The growl had stirred me way down deep and resisting after that? Nope.

Above was a glass-like dome, a huge one, I thought, as he angled his route slightly left. Some sort of multi-winged, fluoro pink bug drifted by in flocks, way up high. And other things bobbed up there, too, transparent, blue, and batting against the glass. Flower petals? If so, those were immense.

Beyond the glass lay deep blackness and bright stars.

"Wow." I said as he slid me to the ground, to land on my feet. My sleek cream dress slipped to mid-calf. My hair was in a single plait, and I had black orc tattoos on both arms now, from wrist to shoulder.

"Those stars would be blurred streaks, if we were still shooting along at the highest WORSK speed, jumping between wormholes." He took my hand, and we strolled through the low shrubs, following a pale path that led toward the center. Kragga the tour guide? I smiled.

The starship was revolving, and slowly a nearby planet rolled into view. Circled and cloaked by cloud, her surface showed a mixture of greens and blues, as well as the white, upper atmosphere.

"*Nodaku*. She's where we mean to trade and do a few missions. We need the work after these weeks of turmoil. Maybe I can get us a ride down that won't be too costly."

"To see another planet? That would be awesome. Though it's less impressive now that I'm here—living on a starship."

Kragga leaned in and said stealthily, beside my ear, "On a starship you helped save from destruction, yes."

"It's not a secret." I swept aside a large leaf.

"It is. It has to be, Char."

We threaded through the green undergrowth until we reached a wide pond. At the edges were grottos with small shelters. Kragga drew us to one. Soft grasses sank under my feet, and I sat on a smooth-carved waveform, that ran from ankle-height to shoulder, like a frozen piece of sea. It was covered by a thick quilt as well as pillows. Some scattered petals made me smile. Had he not said orcs were not romantic?

Above was a roof of the same timber carved into another wave with long perforations following the curves, so that we could glimpse the dome.

Across the pond, a gray horn moved above the vegetation. A land shark was my first guess. I pointed at it, and Kragga laughed.

"That's one of the gardeners. A hinoch, a horned race. They meditate and care for guests and the plants. Not everything here is for prettiness. Some of the plants, their fruits or blossoms, are sought after on various planets."

I inhaled. "It's beautiful and smells like heaven."

"Good." He cleared his throat then pulled me down to lie beside him. "I brought you up here to be romantic, like your Earth movies? Like *Pretty Woman*. Except orcs don't do romance."

"That's about a prostitute." I had heard the aliens researched us before descending and abducting people, but movies were a stretch as a research method.

"Yes, like that. I also watched your porn. Orc and human porn. Orc and elf porn. Human and tentacle monster porn." He stared at the pond. "Are elves real?"

"No. They're only in stories."

"A pity." He sat up to kick some pillows away from his feet, then shucked his heavy boots by toeing them off. "Romance and love and all that. I do mean it, but orcs—"

"Aren't much into love?"

"No." He plopped back down and dragged me to him and between his legs. I rolled my head to look up at him. His tusks were showing due to his evil grin. "But we do like fucking and elf porn."

I thought of punching him, but only lightly since he *was* an orc.

"Are you happy, Char?"

"Very." I snuggled into his body, rested the side of my face on his chest where I could hear his heart—my favorite sound.

"Good."

Blindly, I reached above and found his jaw and then his tusks. I caressed those until he mock-snapped at me, capturing my finger. This starship had come close to ending, and perhaps I had also, but Kragga had swept that away. I had survived because he had cared for me and found help.

"Remember you said orcs liked to find leaders?" I mumbled.

"Yes."

"Well, you led me to do what we needed to do to slow the engine."

"Not the same, girl."

"Huh. Is, too. Even one follower is enough. I'm following you."

He didn't bother answering me and only lightly traced my skin above his collar that I wore.

Slowly, a wonderful serenity descended over us, or perhaps it was just me. His fuck-this attitude made everything less hectic. Unless it was the omega heat? I didn't feel as if that were coming. The doctor had been wrong.

For the first time, I felt it was safe to ask about the friend I'd made on Vedrock's ship.

"Where is the *Social Deviance* now? I made a friend there called Jinx, a human woman. Is there any way to get her off the ship? A Grut form? They seem to organize everything."

"Vedrock *is* Grut. You knew Jinx? We tried to find her. We'll have to tell Gideon. And I don't know where his ship has gone, but this is another reason to track it down."

For revenge? Or to rescue Jinx? I would follow whatever they did, and help them, if I could, except, revenge was never a good reason. I had learned from my mistakes.

Then he kissed me and lifted me higher, and I straddled him. His arousal was obvious and nudging between my legs. His slow, heated kiss was direly glorious and leg-jellifying. I was glad I wasn't standing on my feet.

He broke away from the kiss. "Romance is good." Our warm breaths mingled in that tiny space between our mouths. His kisses were so nice, whether hard or soft, rough or worshiping. I chased his mouth, kissing him back with a light touch and some teasing tongue. Then I rested my forehead on his chest.

"Romance good." Kragga nodded while lying down. "Fucking is better. That's my orc motto. I may brand it on you somewhere."

I snorted, too content to protest. Surely, he joked.

He twisted and freed his cock, pushed my dress to my waist. As he often demanded, I wore no panties. At a single exploratory nudge, then a harder thrust, his cock parted my lips below and slid in. I gasped and moved to lever myself higher, but he trapped me against his chest.

Karagga grunted. "You take me far better than before. Have I taken your ass like Radaka did?"

He knew. My eyes sprang open. "No!"

"I thought not. Hmmm. Ideas."

Oh. Oh crap. The orc's cock was big enough to be an extra in a horror movie. I was not sure of this.

A noise made me twist my neck to stare across the pond and... there were tentacles rising against a red-and-pink flotilla of petals. Tentacles writhing and plunging. Blue ones. Females were giggling then one was held high in the air by more tentacles, while another impaled between her legs. Radaka had made friends. *Good* friends.

My eyebrows shot up, and Kragga's cock seemed to engorge

further. My pussy tightened down, and I felt a gush of wetness then a torrent of warmth.

Kragga sat up, taking me up with him and he twisted me on his lap. I could easily spy on this sexual extravaganza that played out opposite us.

"Two human females and one mauleon? Radaka has been practicing with those tentacles." He sounded awed. "What a pity you aren't an elf."

"Oh!" I smacked his thigh. The fleshy slap resounded.

His face turned grim. "Bad move."

Which was why, a minute later, I was upended over his lap getting thoroughly spanked while he joyfully sang out, *red ass*, with each blow. The warmth seemed to susurrate through me, making my head spin and fade. I was wet, swollen, and thoroughly turned on, long before he stopped, especially since he kept slipping a cone of his fingers inside me.

"Stay on your hands and knees," he said gruffly. "Time for some romance, orc style. Behave or I will invite the alpha gogogian to play with you again."

I stayed, waiting. My pussy was begging to feel the surge and immense size of this orc's cock, even before he entered me. Waves of minor ecstasy peaked and ebbed. I squeaked as he thrust in, and his cock felt as if it were halfway to my throat. I choked and swayed then looked up at the heavens. The dome above held a drifting shape formed by the crimson petals—an enormous see-through heart.

He *must* have asked for that heart, and if he had not, it was still exactly what should be there. Fucking immaculate.

I groaned and swallowed, for there seemed no way for us to fit together any more perfectly, without a gap between us. Flesh inserted in flesh until I could sense the heartbeat in his cock. We were one creature, one lust-driven, gasping, moaning, and panting organism.

Kragga swore and stayed deep, then he bit me with enough force to leave marks and maybe draw blood. The thrill of that small damage was electric. With half my shoulder caught in his fangs and his tusks, he withdrew and rammed into me again. My hands skidded and slipped, and so did my knees.

Wetness slicked down my legs in a syrupy torrent.

Heat. I knew this even as my mind floundered, sinking, drowning in lust.

"Fuck." He grunted and his teeth marked another part of my body—my back, my waist. I groaned and panted, my arms burning as I struggled to stay on my hands and knees and not collapse. He gripped my hair and pulled back my head, forcing me to arch. "Let's put some orc babies inside you."

One hand was in my hair, the other anchored on my butt, and then he slipped his thumb into my ass. "I fuck your cunt until you come and then..." He ground himself around, forcing me low, making me fall forward onto my thighs. My clit squashed into the cloth-padded timber as he continued to grind. "Then after that, we go in here." His thumb shoved higher, and his ass grip became a painful one made of iron.

The next thrust blew my mind into the oblivion of a climax.

KRAGGA

Hours later, after the knotting and the climaxes, after her cries of submission and a lot of spilled come, we had exhausted ourselves. I'd withdrawn from Char and moved us, still naked, to another shelter in Viewpoint One. It seemed best to take her from the flood we'd created. I carried her in my arms, with our clothes and belongings draped over my arm and shoulder

A hinoch brought us some water and food in return for payment and a thank you.

This was peaceful, lying together with my female. Though if every heat was that vigorous, I might need to schedule recovery days. Or order a new cock.

"Now we can watch the stars for a while and talk about how things will be."

"*Mm-hmm.*" Char nuzzled my arm. "How what will be?"

"You know I have forgiven you for wrecking the galaxy, but I doubt others will be as forgiving. We will have to trust that Smorg and the mechlings do not betray us."

"Yes. I don't know anything much about them."

Neither did I, not really. How could any humanoid be sure they completely understood that sentient sword or the mechlings that followed him?

"So far he has been honest, if a little excruciating in his remarks."

"*Hmph*. Smorg is the AI version of bad dad jokes."

"True." I had no idea what she meant. "Either way, you must promise never to again use your powers. You almost died. You were badly injured both times."

"I suppose." She nuzzled my arm again and nibbled.

I grabbed a handful of hair and levered her head back. "Look at me and agree not to use your powers, or tell anyone else about them. Nobody is trustworthy. No one."

Char frowned then grimaced as I tightened my hold. "Okay. I promise. Not even Isolde?"

"No."

"I promise. Though it's sad not to be able to tell her."

"I know it is." I stroked her hair, reassuring her. "It is what it is."

Some things are too big to reveal to the world. We would trust Smorg only because we had to.

She found my hand and brought it to her mouth, kissed my fingers, and snuggled my hand closer.

"I trust you. Say… that heart I saw above us when we made love? Was that your doing?"

"When we made love? No? I did not observe any such heart."

"Damn. I was sure."

"There, there. You must resign yourself to living forever with an unromantic orc."

I grinned. I was pleased she had seen it, but I wasn't breaking the orc code. We were big mean and green, and we fucked. We did not make love.

I also was never telling her of the death of my friend who turned alpha.

Saying that or speaking of love was not necessary. This little Earth female would know of my feelings for her by the words in her own heart, and by my deeds, and my care for her.

I reached across her and into our clothes. I found the item I was looking for.

"I do, however, have this." I held a red metal heart pendant above her. It spun slowly, showing off the engraved words: KRAGGA'S PET. A tiny jewel was the ownership symbol.

"*Oooo*. Pretty."

"I'm glad you like it."

"It's gorgeous."

When she sat up on her elbow, I turned her collar and began to clip the heart to the collar. "This is my gift to you in thanks for saying yes to a threesome with Radaka, tomorrow."

"What?"

I grinned at the shock in her eyes and wrestled her into sitting above me, with her legs straddling my stomach.

"You heard me. Look, already your pussy is dripping and says yes."

"Fuck." Char lay down flat on me, as if that could hide her slipperiness. "I will think on this."

"Of course. Think on this and say yes." And I smacked her cute, lush, and very naked ass, then squashed her to me until she grunted and spluttered. "You know you want this—one in your ass, one in your mouth, while I rail you? See how romantic I am?"

She muttered something to herself. I could not hear it, but I knew she would eventually say yes and make me a very happy orc.

"I may also have elf ears for you to wear."

"Fuck no. Only… *only* if there are no elf ears."

Yesss. I smiled and squeezed her butt.

Then I sneaked a finger inside her. Her wriggle made me decide I had the energy to take her, once more under the stars and the floating blossoms, while the little heart tinkled on her collar.

The next book in the Ravaged series is
VEDROCK

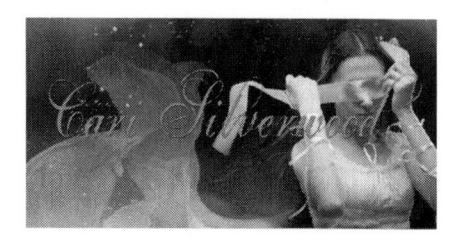

Join my newsletter list to get a free book and find out about releases, teasers, and sales.
https://www.carisilverwood.net/readers-subscribe-page.html

ABOUT THE AUTHOR: CARI SILVERWOOD

I love to hear from my readers.
If you enjoyed Alien Owned, please consider leaving a review on your favorite retailer or website.

Cari Silverwood is a *New York Times* and *USA Today* bestselling writer of kinky darkness or sometimes of dark kinkiness, depending on her moods and the amount of time she's spent staring into the night.

When others are writing bad men doing bad things, you may find her writing good men who accidentally on purpose fall into the abyss and come out with their morals twisted in knots.

Sign up to receive news on releases and sales, and a free welcome book
www.carisilverwood.net/about-me.html
Find Cari on Facebook
www.facebook.com/cari.silverwood

You're welcome to join this group on Facebook to discuss Cari Silverwood's books:
Dark Hearts Discussion Group

ALSO BY CARI SILVERWOOD

Most of my books are in Kindle Unlimited

Recent releases

HIS KEEPSAKE — A dark contemporary romance

WARDEN - Book 1 in the Ravaged series, a Dark Omegaverse Romance

JUDGED — Dark Reverse Harem Sci-fi Romance set in the world of Ruled snd Condemned

SACRIFICED TO THE SEA - A dark mermaid story

CLOCKWORK STALKER – a dark, twisted, Sherlock Holmes and Miss Moriarty romance

RULED – Dark Sci-fi romance

CONDEMNED – Dark Reverse Harem Sci-fi Romance

BEAST HORDE TRILOGY BOXSET

Pierced Hearts Series – contemporary BDSM and dubcon/ noncon series

TAKE ME, BREAK ME

KLAUS – A NOVELLA

BIND AND KEEP ME

MAKE ME YOURS EVERMORE

SEIZE ME FROM DARKNESS

YIELD

THE COMPLETE PIERCED HEARTS BOXSET – all six books in one volume

The Dark Hearts Series – dark romances. Contemporary BDSM and dubcon/ noncon series

WICKED WAYS

WICKED WEAPON

WICKED HUNT

WOLFE – a spin-off novel from the Dark Hearts trilogy

The Possession of Red series (BOOK OF RED) – a spin-off from Dark Hearts

Part 1 USED

Part 2 ISAK & Red

MESMER – a dark romance cowritten with Jennifer Bene and based on my Dark Hearts series

Dark Monster Fantasy Series

PREY

STEEL

BLADE

DARK MONSTER FANTASY BOXSET – pansy-dark scifi romances

Preyfinders Series (alien invasion abduction ROMANCE)

PRECIOUS SACRIFICE

INTIMIDATOR

DEFILER

PREYFINDERS: THE TRILOGY BOXSET

Preyfinders spinoff novel CYBERELLA

The Machinery of Desire Series – dystopian slaveworld series with kink and dubcon/ noncon

ACQUIRED POSSESSION

CLAIMED POSSESSION

FATED POSSESSION – a novella first published in the alien alphas boxset

BRANDED POSSESSION

EXQUISITE POSSESSION

MACHINERY OF DESIRE – THE COMPLETE BOXSET

The Steamwork Chronicles Series

Iron Dominance

Lust Plague

Steel Dominance

THE STEAMWORK CHRONICLES BOXSET – all three books in one volume

The Beast Horde Trilogy – dystopian sci-fi warrior romance

VARGR

RUTGER

CYN

BEAST HORDE TRILOGY BOXSET

Squirm Files Series – tentacle sex spoofs of erotic romance and monster stories

SQUIRM

STRUM

THE WELL-HUNG GUN

SQUIRM FILES SERIES BOXSET

CATACLYSM BLUES

(A free kinky scifi novella)

Others

DARK MATH JESUS – a free satire about how Sacrificed to the Sea ended up in Religion and Math categories.

THE PRINCESS TIED – a kinky fantasy romance. Inspired by The Princess Bride

ROUGH SURRENDER – a BDSM-themed, historical romance set in Cairo in 1910

MY ROMANCE CURSE (erotic romcom)

FAN ANONYMOUS

SANTA WITH A K – A Naughty Xmas Fairy Tale

31 FLAVORS OF KINK (based on a true story)

THREE DAYS OF DOMINANCE

NIGHTMARE RISING – a dark contemporary paranormal story cowritten with Nicolette Hugo

Magience series – epic fantasy

MAGIENCE

NEEDLE RAIN

The Badass Brats Series (contemporary BDSM romances with Mff)

THE DOM WITH A SAFEWORD

THE DOM ON THE NAUGHTY LIST

THE DOM WITH THE PERFECT BRATS

THE DOM WITH THE CLEVER TONGUE

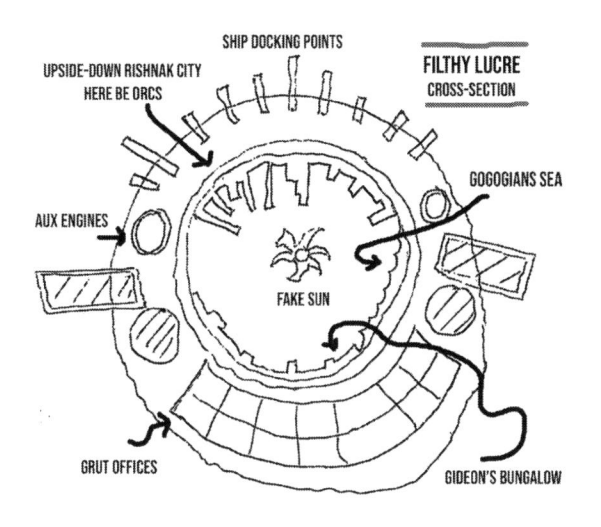

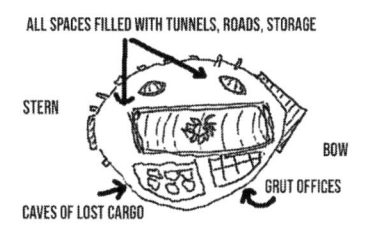

MAP OF THE *FILTHY LUCRE*
A higher resolution version of this bad sketch is on Cari Silverwood's website

GLOSSARY

Terms used in the
Ravaged Omegaverse
Not alphabetical and random as hell

Krak – orc battle/ party music with giant axes, death glares, and screams.

Burning Chaos – the spaceship of Gideon and Kragga. Captained by Laskar, a species with some rat-like features.

Filthy Lucre – The mothership featured in the Ravaged series. Many smaller ships dock onto her and she holds tens of thousands of people.

SMORG - a snarky talking sword, courtesy of programming implanted in its hilt. Made by *GNERSH*.

Awoken mechling – a mechling that is a self-aware AI.

Basja – Orc pre-come and come that induces dilation, attraction, and acceptance in females

Ax-rambler – An orc vehicle. A pastiche of black metal, fins, violent symbols written in red and white, and threatening sharp bits, with all of this wrapped around something akin to a humvee.

Shipmates and Spaceheads and Mercs – Terms for those living and working on starships.

Gogogian – tentacled aliens, normally shorter than humanoids. They love trading, selling stuff to humanoids, finding stuff to sell. They also feed off the good emotions of humanoids.

Grut Soldata - The soldier arm of Grut.

Grut Bureaucracy – A galaxy-wide bureaucracy that does everything in triplicate.

Motherships – Starships that can house thousands of aliens. Smaller ships dock with the mothership.

WORSK engine — wormhole skipping engine used by starships to cross the galaxy

Shipshare – A share of the profits that a spacehead or merc gets from a mission.

Mercenary Guild – The guild of mercs.

Crab Translator – A tracking device implanted below the nape of abducted humans. It's also a translation device.

Space fuel – Hard liquor.

Gruxhyde – A Grut main planet.

The Processors – main AI unit of the Grut Bureaucracy on Gruxhyde.

Social Deviance – a bigger ship though smaller than a mothership. It belongs to Grut.

Wardog – reference to merc spaceships that engaged in war and conflicts.

Hinoch – a horned, rhino-like race. Given to peace and tea ceremonies. They have four fingers, a horn, and gray skin.

Viewport One – a quiet garden on the exterior of *Filthy Lucre* that is beneath a dome.

Rishnak City – city on the mothership, Filthy Lucre, where orcs live. Sometimes called the Upside-down City.

Caves of Lost Cargo – storage area within the tunnel system on *Filthy Lucre*.

The Curse of Big Systems - The bigger they get, the bigger the curse. They all end up overbearing, inefficient, and vaguely villainous. Especially Grut.

Manufactured by Amazon.ca
Bolton, ON